Eight
SCANDALOUS...

THE

Balfour
LEGACY

Scandal on the night of the world-famous one hundredth Balfour
Charity Ball has left the Balfour family in disarray! Proud
patriarch Oscar Balfour knows that something must be done.
His only option is to cut his daughters off from their lavish life-
styles and send them out into the real world to stand on
their own two feet. So he dusts off the Balfour family rules and
uses his powerful contacts to place each girl in a situation that
will challenge her particular personality. He is determined that
each of his daughters should learn that money will not
buy happiness—integrity, decorum, strength, trust…and
love are everything!

Each month Mills & Boon® is delighted to bring you an exciting
new instalment from **The Balfour Legacy**.
You won't want to miss out!

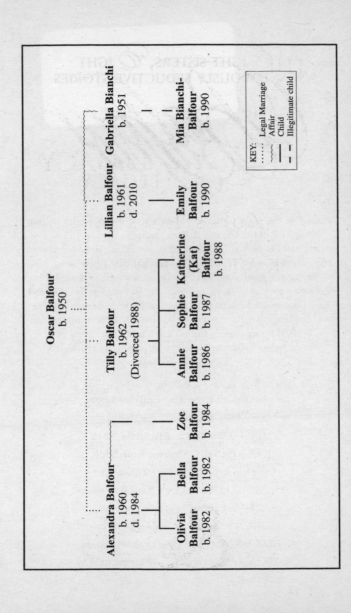

Oscar Balfour
b. 1950

Alexandra Balfour
b. 1960
d. 1984

Tilly Balfour
b. 1962
(Divorced 1988)

Lillian Balfour
b. 1961
d. 2010

Gabriella Bianchi
b. 1951

Olivia Balfour
b. 1982

Bella Balfour
b. 1982

Zoe Balfour
b. 1984

Annie Balfour
b. 1986

Sophie Balfour
b. 1987

Katherine (Kat) Balfour
b. 1988

Emily Balfour
b. 1990

Mia Bianchi-Balfour
b. 1990

KEY:
...... : Legal Marriage
∿∿∿ : Affair
—— : Child
– – : Illegitimate child

THE

Balfour
LEGACY

Zoe's Lesson

KATE HEWITT

MILLS & BOON

First published in Great Britain 2010. This edition 2011.
Mills & Boon, an imprint of Harlequin (UK) Limited,
Eton House, 18-24 Paradise Road, Richmond, Surrey TW9 1SR

ZOE'S LESSON © by Harlequin Books SA 2010

Special thanks and acknowledgement are given to Kate Hewitt for her
contribution to The Balfour Legacy series.

ISBN: 978 0 263 89643 5

022-1211

Harlequin (UK) policy is to use papers that are natural, renewable and
recyclable products and made from wood grown in sustainable forests. The
logging and manufacturing processes conform to the legal environmental
regulations of the country of origin.

Printed and bound in Spain
by Blackprint CPI, Barcelona

Kate Hewitt discovered her first Mills & Boon® romance on a trip to England when she was thirteen and she's continued to read them ever since.

She wrote her first story at the age of five, simply because her older brother had written one and she thought she could do it too. That story was one sentence long—fortunately, they've become a bit more detailed as she's grown older.

She has written plays, short stories and magazine serials for many years, but writing romance remains her first love. Besides writing, she enjoys reading, travelling and learning to knit.

After marrying the man of her dreams—her older brother's childhood friend—she lived in England for six years and now resides in Connecticut with her husband, her three young children and the possibility of one day getting a dog.

Kate loves to hear from readers—you can contact her through her website, www.kate-hewitt.com.

Don't miss Kate's latest book, *The Lone Wolfe,* part of the BAD BLOOD series! Out now!

To Maggie, a great New York friend!
Love, K.

CHAPTER ONE

MAX MONROE gazed at the cherry blossoms outside the doctor's office on Park Avenue, the fully opened buds as soft and round as pink puffballs. He blinked; were the blossoms blurring together into one indiscernible rosy mass, or was he imagining it? Fearing it?

He turned back to the doctor who was smiling at him with far too much compassion and steepled his fingers under his chin. When he spoke his voice was bland, deliberately so. 'So what are we looking at? A year?' He swallowed. 'Six months?'

'It's difficult to say.' Dr Ayers glanced down at the clipboard that chronicled Max's history of sight loss in a few clinical sentences. 'Stargardt's disease is not a predictable process. As you know, many are diagnosed in childhood, yet yours was not detected until recently.' He gave a tiny, apologetic shrug. 'You could have months of blurred vision, loss of central vision, sudden blackouts…' He paused, tellingly.

'Or?' Max asked, the single word opening up a well of unwelcome possibility.

'Or it could be faster than that. You might have nearly complete loss of sight within a few weeks.'

'Weeks.' Max repeated the word with cold detachment,

turning to gaze once more at the blowsy blossoms, now at the height of their glory. Perhaps he wouldn't see them fall, wouldn't witness the silky pink petals turn brown and wrinkled, curling up at the corners before they fluttered slowly, disconsolately to the ground.

Weeks.

'Max—'

Max held up a hand to stop the doctor's words of sympathy. He didn't want to hear how sorry the man was, how Max didn't deserve this. Polite but pointless offerings. 'Please,' he said quietly, his throat suddenly—stupidly—tight.

Dr Ayers shook his head, his words lapsing into a sigh. 'Your case is unique, as the head trauma from your accident might have exacerbated or even accelerated the conditions of the disease. Many people with this disease can live with a managed condition—'

'While others are legally blind and have nearly complete loss,' Max finished dispassionately. He'd done his research, back when the first flickers of darkness rippled across his vision, as if the world had gone wavy. Back when he'd been able to read, watch, *see*. Just three weeks ago, yet a separate lifetime.

The doctor sighed again, then reached for a brochure. 'Living with sight loss is challenging—'

Max gave a sharp bark of disbelieving laughter. Challenging? He could *do* challenging. He thrived on challenges. Sight loss was not a challenge. It was a devastation. Darkness, utter darkness, as he'd felt once before, when the fear had consumed him, when he'd heard their cries— He bit off that train of thought, refused to lose himself in the memories. It would be all too easy, and then he would never find his way back.

'I could refer you to some groups that help you to become accustomed—'

'No.' He pushed the proffered brochure away and forced himself to meet the doctor's compassionate gaze, angling his head so the man's blurred face was in his peripheral vision, where his eyesight was best. He blinked, as though that would help. As though it would change. Already the world was losing its focus, softening and darkening at the edges like an old photograph. Shapes blurred, and spots and lights drifted across his vision, like stars in a darkening sky. How much he could see at any given time was, as Max was coming to realise, a complete crap shoot.

And when he was sightless, Max wondered, when the curtain of his vision finally drew completely closed, would the present reality—those vibrant cherry blossoms—be like an old photograph to him too? Blurred and distant, hard to remember, fading with time? How would he cope with the unending darkness? He'd felt it once before; he couldn't bear to face it again, yet there was no choice. No choice at all.

He shook his head, both to block the thought and Dr Ayers's suggestion. 'I'm not interested in joining some kind of group,' he said flatly. 'I'll handle this my own way.'

'I'm not talking about some touchy-feely thing—' Dr Ayers began. He was, Max knew, a military man, which is why he'd been referred to him. Army, though, not air force. And he hadn't seen any action.

'I know.' He forced his lips to stretch into a meaningless smile. 'Thank you.' He rose from his chair, his head aching, his leg throbbing with pain. For a moment he felt dizzy, groundless, and he reached out to steady himself on the corner of the doctor's desk. He missed, his hand swiping through air, and he cursed aloud.

'Max—'

'I'm fine.' He righted himself, shoulders thrown back in military fashion, his eyes dark and hard, the scar that now bisected his face, running from the inside corner of his right eyebrow along the side of his nose to the curl of his lip, blazing with remembered feeling. Pain. 'Thank you,' he said again and, walking with careful, deliberate steps, he left the office.

Outside the window a single, silky petal fluttered lazily to the ground.

Zoe Balfour handed her wrap—nothing more than a bit of spangled silk—to the woman at the coat-check counter and ran a hand through her artfully tousled hair. Throwing back her shoulders, she stood for a moment in the soaring entrance of the Soho loft and waited for heads to turn. She needed heads to turn, shamelessly craved the attention and praise. She needed to feel like she always had, as though her world hadn't blown apart when the newspapers had splashed the story of her illegitimate birth across their pages just three weeks ago. When the world—her world—had drawn a collective gasp of salacious shock. When she realised she didn't know who she was any more.

She took a deep breath and entered the art gallery, plucking a glass of champagne from a nearby tray and taking a deep draught. She relished the crisp taste of it on her tongue, the bubbles zinging through her body. And she saw—and felt—the heads turn, but realised now she didn't know why they were turning. Was it because she was a beautiful woman entering a party, or because they knew who she was—and who she wasn't?

Zoe took another sip of champagne, as if the alcohol could ward off the despair that stole coldly into her soul despite her intent to have fun, to forget. It frayed the edges of her composure, made her feel as if she were teetering on the precipice of something terrible, an abyss she couldn't even fathom or name. It was a despair and a fear she'd been fighting since the newspapers had told the story of her shame, and even more so since she arrived in New York three days ago, at the request of her father. No, Zoe mentally corrected, not her father. Oscar Balfour, the man who had raised her.

Her father was here in New York.

Only that afternoon she'd finally summoned her courage to stand outside the gleaming skyscraper on Fifty-Seventh Street, watching and waiting for a glimpse of the man she'd come here to see. She'd paced; she'd drunk three coffees; she'd even bitten her nails. After two hours he still hadn't appeared and she'd slunk back to the Balfour penthouse on Park Avenue, feeling like an impostor, a fake and a cheat.

Because she *wasn't* a Balfour.

For twenty-six years she'd smugly rested in the knowledge that she was one of the Balfour girls, a member of one of the oldest, wealthiest and most powerful families in all of England, if not all of Europe. And then she'd learned— from the front page of a gossip rag, no less—that she had not a drop of Balfour blood in her veins.

She was nobody, nothing. A bastard.

'Zoe!' Her friend Karen Buongornimo, the organiser of tonight's gallery opening, looking sleek and elegant in a little—tiny actually—black number, her hair like a gleaming dark waterfall, pressed a powdered cheek to hers. 'You look amazing, as I knew you would. Are you ready to sparkle?'

'Of course.' Zoe smiled, her voice airy and bright.

Perhaps she was the only one to notice its brittle edge. 'Sparkle is what I do best.'

'Absolutely.' Karen gave her shoulder a little squeeze and Zoe tried to inject some feeling into her smile. Her face hurt with the effort. 'I'm just about to make some terribly insipid remarks—I have to thank our sponsors, including Max Monroe.' Karen rolled her eyes suggestively, and Zoe raised her eyebrows, trying to act as if the name had meaning for her. 'He's apparently the most eligible bachelor in the city, but he's certainly not winning any points from me tonight.'

'Oh?' Zoe took another sip of champagne. Someone else wasn't having a good time, she thought, even as another part of her brain insisted fiercely that she *was* having a good time—she was the good-time girl. An accident of birth didn't need to change that.

Because if it did...

'No, he's sulking—or really, glowering—in a corner, looking like he's got a thundercloud over his head. Not exactly approachable.' Karen pouted prettily. 'He's probably consumed a magnum of champagne on his own.' She gave a little sigh. 'Still, he is rather sexy...I think the scar just adds to it, don't you?'

'I'm afraid I don't see the man in question,' Zoe replied, surveying the milling crowd, her curiosity piqued, and Karen shrugged.

'It won't be hard to miss him. He's the one looking like someone's torturing him. He *did* have an accident a month or so ago, and he's not been the same since. *Such* a nuisance.' She shrugged again and set her glass on an empty tray, air-kissing Zoe on both cheeks. 'All right, I must get everyone's attention somehow.' She pulled her designer dress down a bit, to reveal another inch of bronzed cleavage, and gave Zoe a salacious wink. 'Shouldn't be too hard.'

Smiling faintly, Zoe took another sip of champagne and watched her friend work the crowd. *She* was usually the one working the crowd, yet she found she couldn't summon the energy or even the desire to chat and flirt and *sparkle*. All it seemed she could do was remember.

Illegitimacy Scandal Rocks Balfour Legacy!
When Blue Blood Turns Bad!

The newspaper headlines screamed inside her mind ever since a grasping journalist had overheard her sisters' argument at the Balfour Charity Ball. They'd discovered the truth of Zoe's birth in her mother's forgotten journal, and Zoe wished they'd never opened that worn book, wished she could forget the truth that now would never escape her. Bad blood. *Her* blood.

The shame and pain of it was too much to endure or even consider, and so she hadn't. She'd accepted every invitation, gone to every party and nightclub, in an attempt to forget the shame of her own birth, her own self. She'd found her wildest friends and acted as if she didn't care. Yet all the while she'd been frozen, numb. Wonderfully numb.

Oscar had let her be for a fortnight, hardly ever home, arriving at dawn only to sleep the day away.

Then he'd finally forced her out of bed and called her into his study, that sanctum of burnished mahogany and soft leather, the smell of pipe tobacco lingering in the air. She'd always loved that room with its unabashed masculinity and its memories of Sunday afternoons curled into her father's deep leather armchair, flipping through his old atlases and encyclopedias, reading and dreaming of faraway places, exotic names and plants and animals. She'd never been much of a student at boarding school, but she'd loved to read those fusty old books and then regale her family with odd little facts nobody expected her to know.

Yet that afternoon in her father's study she hadn't even glanced at the row of embossed leather encyclopedias. She'd simply stood by the door, listless and blank faced and a bit hungover.

'Zoe.' Her father swivelled in his desk chair to survey her with a kind-hearted compassion that made Zoe's insides shrivel. It looked—and felt—like the compassion of a pitying stranger, not the deserved emotion of a father. 'This can't go on.'

She swallowed, her throat tight, and forced her shoulders to give a tiny shrug. Her head ached. 'I don't know what—'

'Zoe.' He spoke more firmly, giving her a stern stare that reminded her of when she'd been eight years old and had got into her stepmother's make-up. She'd used most of a lipstick and eyeshadow in one sitting, and somehow managed to make it to school decked out in glittery warpaint without anyone noticing. 'For the last fortnight you've been out all hours, God knows who with, doing what—'

'I'm twenty-six years old,' Zoe returned sulkily. 'I can do as I like—'

'Not in my house, with my money.' Although his tone was level, there was a hardness in Oscar's eyes that made Zoe stare at her feet, more miserable than ever before. 'I know the story in that rubbishy newspaper upset you,' he continued more gently, 'but—'

'It's not a story.'

For a second Oscar looked nonplussed. 'Pardon?'

'It's not a story,' Zoe repeated a bit more loudly. She looked up, staring at her father with the angry challenge of a sulky child—except she wasn't a child, had never been *his* child. 'It's the truth.'

Oscar was silent for a long moment, too long. 'Oh, Zoe,' he finally said, shaking his head, 'is that what you think? That…that somehow this matters?'

'Of course it matters,' she'd replied, her voice torn between a hiss and a whisper. 'It matters to *me*.'

'Well, I can assure you it doesn't matter to me,' Oscar replied briskly. 'If the truth must be told, Zoe, I suspected as much from before you were born—'

'What?' Zoe recoiled as if she'd been stung. Hurt. 'You *knew*?'

'I suspected,' Oscar replied evenly. 'Your mother and I—well, we hadn't been happy together in some time—'

'You knew all this time and you never thought to tell me?' Zoe shook her head, blinking back angry tears.

'Zoe,' Oscar asked gently, 'why would I tell you such a thing? You are—and always have been—my child in every way that matters.'

Zoe could only shake her head again, unable to voice the clamour of unsettling emotions that raced through her. How could she explain to her father that it wasn't the same, that it *did* matter? She wasn't a Balfour. She didn't belong.

'I know,' Oscar continued quietly, his voice laced with his own sorrow, 'this is difficult for you. In a matter of months you've lost your stepmother, and discovered you have another sister—'

'But I don't.' Zoe met her father's gaze directly. 'Mia's no blood relation to me.' It hurt to say it. Only in the past few weeks had she—and the rest of her sisters—discovered Oscar's affair before he married Lillian, and the daughter that had resulted from the one-night liaison. Yet while Mia had discovered she was a Balfour, Zoe had learned she was not. The irony tasted bitter in her mouth.

'This isn't about blood,' Oscar said a bit sharply. 'I

know I've made my mistakes over the years, Zoe, but surely you know I've loved you and been a father to you.'

Tears pricked her eyes and she averted her face. 'But I'm not a Balfour.'

Oscar was silent for a long moment, long enough for Zoe to fidget uncomfortably, afraid she'd said something too revealing.

'I see,' he finally said, and he sounded almost disappointed. 'It's simply about the name. Are you worried how people might see you? Judge you?'

Heat rushed into her face and she turned back to him. 'So what if I am? You're not the one whose photograph is being splashed about on the pages of every gossip rag—'

'Actually, Zoe, I am, along with you and your sisters.' Oscar sighed. 'My mistakes are being proclaimed to the world, and I am learning to hold my head high in spite of them. I hope you can hold yours high too, for your last name or even the blood running through your veins doesn't change who you *are*.' Zoe said nothing. She couldn't reply because in her mind it did.

Growing up she'd always felt different, as if she didn't belong somehow. She'd thought it was simply because Bella and Olivia were twins; they had a bond that no one else could break or match. Or perhaps it was because she was the only one without any memories of her mother, since Alexandra had died in childbirth. *Her* birth. Emily had Lillian, whom everyone had loved; Kat, Sophie and Annie had their mother, Tilly, who was beloved by the other girls as well.

Zoe had no one. No mother she could call her own.

And now she knew why she'd felt so separate. It was this. She really *didn't* belong. It wasn't just a feeling; it was the truth.

'I'd like you to go to New York,' Oscar said, withdrawing a leather wallet from the drawer. Inside Zoe glimpsed a first-class plane ticket. 'You can stay in the apartment there as long as you like.'

She took the wallet, her fingers digging into the soft leather. 'Why do you want me to go?' she asked, although she heard the question underneath: *Why do you want me to leave?*

Oscar sighed wearily and rubbed his eyes. 'I read your mother's journal myself, Zoe, and from the things she's written, I have a good idea of who—' He paused, and when he spoke again his voice sounded sorrowful. 'Who your biological father might be.'

Zoe stiffened, froze. 'You know? *Who?*'

Oscar waved a hand towards the wallet. 'The details are in there. But he's in New York, and I think it will help you to know...and perhaps even to find him.' He paused, his smile gentle and touched with sorrow. 'You're stronger than you think, Zoe.'

Yet she hadn't felt strong then, and she didn't now. She felt appallingly, pathetically weak, too weak even to look for the man she'd come to find. Too weak and afraid to even talk to anyone at this party; every outing frayed her composure, her sense of self, a bit more, until she was left clutching the ragged edges, feeling as if she had nothing, was nothing.

Who was she? Who could she be now?

Another sip of champagne, Dutch courage. God knew, she didn't have any of the real kind.

Max surveyed the milling crowd in the art gallery, a mass of bright, blurred shapes. Had his vision worsened in the few hours since his doctor's appointment, or was it simply psychological? His mind, bent with fear, making him think

he really was seeing less? Although if vision were simply
a matter of will, surely he would see perfectly by now. He
wanted nothing more.

He took a sip of champagne, one shoulder propped
against the metal pillar of the soaring loft space, its walls
decked with nouveau art that fortunately really were just
blobs of colour.

He hadn't wanted to come tonight; the only reason he
had was because his company, Monroe Consulting, had
donated an embarrassingly large amount towards this ex-
hibition. Glancing at the walls, Max wasn't sure why he'd
allowed a quarter million dollars to fund what looked like
really appallingly bad art, but he supposed it hardly
mattered. Someone on his board had made the decision
months ago, and he'd signed off on it because he hadn't
much cared. He'd been too busy with his life, with
managing his company, flying his plane and finding the
next beautiful woman to grace his arm. All those pursuits,
he acknowledged grimly, would soon be denied to him, one
way or another. Some, like flying, were already. For the rest
it was simply a matter of time.

'*Max.*' A woman pressed his hand with both of hers, and
he inhaled her cloyingly floral scent. She dropped her voice
to a breathy whisper. '*So* good of you to come. Considering…' She trailed off delicately, but Max wasn't in a mood
to let her off the hook. He couldn't quite make out her
features but the nauseating perfume and the deliberate
whisper told him all he needed to know. This was Letitia
Stephens, one of New York's most prominent aging social-
ites, and a notoriously vicious gossip.

He arched an eyebrow and offered his most urbane
smile. 'Considering what, Letitia?'

A tiny pause, and she withdrew her hands from his,

shifting her weight in a slightly discomfited manner. 'Oh, Max.' This was said almost reproachfully, and Max just smiled and waited. 'Everyone has been so worried for you…since the *accident*…'

Suddenly Max's moment of good humour—or something close to it—evaporated. He'd walked right into that one, but he still didn't want to be reminded of his accident…the smoke, the sudden darkness. The spiralling into nothingness, the agonising understanding of just what had happened. The pain and the memory. No, he didn't want to remember.

He straightened, his body stiffening, shoulders back, a position he wore like armour, remembered not only from his years in the military, but from childhood.

Stand up straight. Take it like a man.

'Thank you for your concern.' He said it as a dismissal, and Letitia Stephens was—for once—wise enough to accept it as such. Max was glad he couldn't see well enough to catch the murderous glare she was undoubtedly favouring him with, the poisonously saccharin smile. He turned away, not wanting to invite another conversation.

Alone, he tossed back the last of his champagne and debated leaving. It wasn't even nine o'clock, and the organiser of tonight's party, a glamorous socialite named Karen Buongornimo—all he'd seen was a flash of dark hair and the gleam of an artificially whitened smile—had yet to speak. He would be publicly thanked; he needed to stay. This would, he determined, be the last such event he attended. It wasn't simply difficult to navigate the sea of blurred faces and bodies; it was dangerous and humiliating. He did not intend to endure it another time. Grimacing, he held out his glass for a refill.

* * *

Zoe skirted the edge of the crowd, clutching her champagne, avoiding conversations. She watched as Karen called for everyone's attention, and half listened as she gave a flowery speech about the importance of supporting emerging artists and how Monroe Consulting had been so fabulously generous. Monroe Consulting…that must be Max Monroe's firm. The man with the thundercloud. Zoe felt another little dart of curiosity. She tossed back the rest of her champagne. Tonight was not a night for thinking. Or remembering.

Tonight she was going to have fun. She was good at that; she'd always been good at that. And now it helped her to forget.

'And I'm sure Max Monroe would like to say a few words…' Zoe didn't so much as hear Karen's introduction as the deafeningly awkward silence after it. Heads turned, bodies swivelling, waiting for the man in question to speak.

He didn't.

Zoe craned her neck, standing on tiptoes in her already stiletto heels, but there were too many people—not to mention a large concrete pillar—for her to see the dreaded Max.

Finally, when the silence had gone on long enough for Karen to look both annoyed and embarrassed, and several people had cleared their throats in a telling manner, he spoke.

'I have one word.' His voice was low, his tone dry, almost, Zoe thought with a pang of recognition, bitter. 'Cheers.'

Another silence, and then someone called out, 'Hear, hear!' and a peal of laughter like staccato gunfire burst out, the tension easing. No one wanted the party to be ruined, it seemed.

'Cheers,' Zoe said aloud, and reached for another glass of champagne.

She might not be a Balfour any more, but she could still act like one.

She surveyed the crowd; she recognised most people, knew only a few. Good. It was better that way. Tonight she wanted to laugh and forget the burden of her birth. She wanted to have *fun*.

'Drowning your sorrows, darling?'

Zoe froze. She knew that voice, hated that voice. She turned slowly, hardly able to believe who she was seeing… Holly Mabberly, her nemesis from boarding school and the it-crowd in London. They weren't enemies, precisely. Nothing so uncivilised. In fact, most people probably thought they were friends. They air-kissed and chatted in public, laughed in perfect trills and fetched each other drinks. During one winter evening Holly had even borrowed her new pashmina when they'd decided to walk to another party. Zoe wasn't sure she'd ever returned it.

Yet she would never call Holly her friend. She remembered in year four at Westfields, when a scholarship girl had been caught filching lipsticks from the chemist's in the village, and had been expelled. Holly had smiled a terribly cold smile and said, 'Well, that's a relief.'

Zoe didn't know why that seemingly insignificant moment had stuck with her, why that smile had chilled her to the bone, the offhand, callous remark cutting deep. Yet it had. For in Holly's arctic gaze she sensed a predatory anticipation, an eagerness to see the high brought low.

And this was surely the moment she'd been waiting for, for Zoe had been brought very low indeed.

Zoe hesitated a split second before taking a final sip of her drink, draining its dregs. Then she lifted her head, tilting her chin as she deposited her glass on a nearby tray.

'What sorrows, Holly?' she asked sweetly. 'I'm having the time of my life.'

Holly's mouth turned delicately down at the corners in a perfected expression of false compassion. She reached out to clasp Zoe's bare arm with her hand, her fingernails digging into the tender skin. 'You don't need to pretend with me, Zoe. I know—well, actually I can't know, as I'm not...*you know*—but I can only imagine how you feel absolutely—' she paused, searching for the word before latching onto it with relish '—*destroyed.*' She squeezed her fingers again as she added sadly, 'Completely lost.'

Zoe blinked, surprised by Holly's inadvertent perception, for that was exactly how she felt. Lost, spinning in a great void of unknowing, the ground she'd thought so solid under her feet not simply shifted but *gone*. She blinked again, refocusing on Holly, her blue eyes narrowed to assessing slits, her mouth still curved in a smile that didn't even bother masquerading as anything but malice.

'Lost?' she repeated with a little laugh. She choked on the sound; it wasn't her perfect trill. More like a wobble. 'Good gracious, Holly, you're sounding awfully melodramatic. Why should I feel lost? I think the only time I felt that way was when we tried to walk back from the Oxford-Cambridge boat race—do you remember?' She laughed again, and this time the sound rang true—or rather false—a perfect crystalline peal. 'It took us four hours to make it from Putney Bridge to Mayfair. Too many drinks, I suppose.'

'Darling.' Holly squeezed her arm, her nails digging in deeper. Zoe bit the inside of her cheek to keep from wincing. 'I told you, you don't need to pretend with me.' She dropped her voice to a whisper that still managed to carry to seemingly every corner of the room. 'Is it just too, too awful? Is that why you came to New York? To get away from all the gossip, the whispers and stares?' Holly made a moue, the expression of sympathy so patently false it made Zoe's skin crawl.

'I'm fine, Holly,' she managed to say, but her voice sounded wooden. It had been three weeks since the Charity Ball, but this was the first person who had dared to openly confront her about the tabloid's story in all that time, the first person whose scorn and relish she had to face, and of course it had to be Holly Mabberly. Yet it hardly mattered; there were dozens of Holly Mabberlys in the world, in her life, people who would act just the same as she was, disguising scorn with sympathy. She shook Holly's arm off, giving her an icy smile. 'So sorry to disappoint you, as I'm sure you'd prefer me in floods of tears, but really, I'm fine.'

Holly just shook her head. 'Oh, darling, you don't need to take it out on *me*.' This was said with the perfect combination of reproach and pity that had Zoe swallowing a molten lump of fury. Holly patted her cheek. 'I can only imagine how utterly difficult it must be. You can hardly hold your head up in England any more, can you? Not amongst anyone who matters anyway.' Holly clucked her tongue, and this time her voice carried all too well. 'It's too, too sad. I suppose blood will out, though, won't it?'

To her horror Zoe found her eyes suddenly filling with tears. *Stupid.* Holly's remarks were childish and aimed to wound; how could she let them? And how could she cry *here*? She wanted to hold her head high and proud, as Oscar had said. She *did*. She just wasn't sure she could. She wasn't strong, no matter what he thought.

She could not, would not, cry now, not in front of Holly Mabberly, who would gloat and tell every soul and socialite from here to Paris, not in a room full of strangers who suddenly seemed no more than a gang of nosy eavesdroppers. Not here. Please, not here. She hadn't cried since she'd learned the news; she'd kept it together, her composure all too fragile but still intact. Why on earth would she break down in the middle of a party?

She'd been having fun, for heaven's sake.

'Oh, Zoe…' Holly murmured, reaching out again, but Zoe avoided her grasping claw and took a stumbling step backwards.

'Leave me alone, Holly. Just leave me alone.' The last came out in a strangled sob that made Zoe close her eyes in an agony of humiliation. She spun away from Holly, reaching wildly for another glass of champagne—anything to forget that wretched moment, her whole wretched, false life.…

Half hiding behind a pillar, a few deep breaths—and sips—later, the threat of tears had mercifully receded and Zoe felt more like herself, although, she acknowledged, she hardly knew who that person was any more.

She surveyed the crowd, conscious of a new crop of speculative looks, a sly ripple of curious murmurs. Was everyone looking at her, or was she just imagining it in a fit of humiliated paranoia? If she left now, would it be so obvious that she was running away…again?

Her gaze fastened on a man in a corner of the room, his shoulder propped against a pillar, a glass of champagne in his hand. He was incredibly good-looking, with dark, cropped hair, olive skin and a towering physique that did more than justice to the expensive navy suit he wore. Yet it was the look on his face that appealed to Zoe; he looked beyond bored, totally uninterested in the party or anyone there, and the thought filled her with a strange, dizzy relief.

Here was a man who wasn't going to slip sly innuendoes into the conversation; he looked as if he didn't want to talk at all. He certainly didn't want to be noticed, and he hadn't noticed her. Yet.

She ran a hand through her tousled hair, took a deep breath and straightened the silky jade-green halter top she wore. Smile now firmly in place, she sauntered over to the one man in the room she was quite sure had no interest in Zoe Balfour.

Perhaps, she thought, he would be interested in just Zoe.

CHAPTER TWO

HE DIDN'T see her coming; he felt it. A sudden charge in the atmosphere, a ripple in the air, like an electric current wired straight to his heart. The jolt reverberated through him and the little hairs on the nape of his neck prickled with awareness as his fingers instinctively clenched around his drink.

Please, no more pity.

'Hello, there.' Her voice was pleasantly low, pitched to an inviting huskiness. Max thought he detected an English accent, which became more pronounced when she spoke again. 'I had to come over here to see if you are as bored as you look.'

'Even more so,' he returned a bit flatly. He turned his head to look at her, at least as much as he could. He saw a sweep of golden hair, the smooth, pale curve of a cheek and the glitter of green—her eyes as well as her top. She smelled faintly of rose water. His gut clenched with an unexpected spasm of desire.

'Oh, dear. That *is* bad,' she returned with a little laugh that sounded like the tinkling of crystal bells. 'Will another drink cure it, do you think?'

'I've had too many already.' His voice came out brusque

again; he couldn't help it. What was the point in encouraging this little flirtation? If she knew...

'Well, I haven't.' He saw her raise her arm, slender and pale, and soon a waiter hurried over. She plucked a glass from the tray and, turning back to him, took a sip. 'If you're so monumentally bored, why did you come this evening?'

'Because my company donated a quarter of a million dollars to fund these monstrosities on the walls.'

She paused for a tiny second, and then gave an abrupt and unpractised laugh; it was a wonderfully throaty gurgle, so different from her earlier calculated peal. His gut clenched again, and he found himself wondering if her hair was as soft as it smelled, if a smell could even be considered soft. His other senses, he realised, were heightened by his lack of sight. Was the faint smell of roses a perfume or soap? He inhaled it every time she moved, faint and yet so temptingly evocative.

'Oh, of course,' she said, her voice still filled with laughter. 'You're Max Monroe. The one with the thundercloud.'

'That's the first time I've heard that,' he replied drily. For the first time in weeks he was enjoying himself, or close enough. He was actually not remembering.

'Well, you haven't exactly been the life and soul of the party, have you?' she said, and he felt her shrug, felt the slippery feel of her silk top against her silken skin. How he could feel it, he didn't know; he certainly couldn't see it. Yet even though his eyes saw little more than blurred shapes, a bit sharper at the edges, his body felt something else. Every part of him prickled with awareness, with longing.

He *wanted* her.

He hadn't been with a woman since his accident, hadn't felt another's touch except for the cool, clinical hands of a doctor, and now suddenly he craved it. Needed to be close to someone, to breathe her scent and feel her skin. And more than that. To move with her, inside her. To ease the emptiness, to not be alone.

Even if it couldn't go anywhere, even if only for a night. Even if it was with one of society's shallow darlings, as she surely must be.

'I don't suppose I need to be the life and soul of this party,' he finally said, 'with guests like you to give it some energy.' He knew her type, knew what kind of beautiful, confident woman walked over to a strange—and sulking—man and asked him for a drink. It was the kind of woman he pursued, the kind of woman he'd always wanted.

And he wanted her now. She didn't need to know he was almost blind; she wouldn't even stay the night. He'd make sure of that.

He felt her tense for a tiny moment, felt it like a shiver in the air. Then she shrugged and took another sip of champagne. 'I can't deny I like to have fun,' she said lightly.

He shifted his weight; his leg, still recovering from the accident, was starting to hurt. 'Are you having fun tonight?'

She gave another practised laugh. 'No, I think I'm as bored as you are. I'm just better at not showing it.'

'Right, I'm the one with the thundercloud.' He arched an eyebrow. 'What is that supposed to mean?'

'My friend Karen organised this event,' she explained, her tone breezy. 'She was rather put out at how unhelpful you've been, you know. She said I'd recognise you by the thundercloud over your head. And of course—' She stopped suddenly and, even though he couldn't really see her, Max's eyes narrowed.

'And?' he asked softly.

She paused. 'The scar,' she said quietly. She lifted her hand and for a moment Max thought she was going to touch him. He didn't move. Her hand—he could tell it was pale and slender, at least—hovered in the air for a moment before she dropped it back to her side. He felt as if everything had suddenly changed, the light, flirtatious banter turning dark and intimate and far too intense. He didn't want her pity, yet he craved her touch. 'I suppose it's a bit like the elephant in the room,' she said, her voice quiet, rueful and perhaps a little sad. 'No one ever talks about it. Were you in a car accident or something?'

'Something.' Although he spoke tersely, Max felt a reluctant flicker of admiration for her candour. So few people he knew actually told him the truth, unvarnished and unpalatable. He was surrounded by sycophants and social climbers who only told him what they thought he wanted to hear.

And doctors. Doctors at least told him the truth.

'I'm sorry anyway,' she said quietly, and he could tell she meant it. She surprised him, and he didn't want to be surprised. It was easier when she was shallow, when he could believe she was shallow. He wanted a bed partner, not a soulmate. It was too late for that, too late for him.

They were both silent for a moment, and Max wondered if she would walk away. *He* should walk away; he would, except he was afraid he might bump into a pillar or a waiter or God knew what else. He hadn't expected that unguarded moment, hadn't wanted it. Had he? She was a shallow, beautiful socialite; she'd said as much, and he wanted to take her at face value.

To take her, and then leave her, for surely he had no other choice.

'So,' he said, and pitched his voice to a low, sensual hum that had her leaning closer to hear him. He breathed in the rose-water scent again. 'Are you really as bored by this party as I am?' There could be no mistaking his innuendo or his intent.

She was silent for a long moment, and he turned so their faces were close, so he could look directly at her, or as directly as he could, in the periphery of his vision. And for a moment, despite the floaters and spots and blurs, he felt he saw perfectly. Her eyes were vivid green, her mouth a perfect pink curve. She was smiling.

'Yes,' she said softly, 'I think I am.'

Resolve fired through him. 'Good,' he said, placing his empty glass on a tray. 'Then why don't we both get out of here?'

Zoe watched as Max started stiffly from his corner; he walked with careful, deliberate steps that made her wonder if he'd hurt himself in whatever 'something' had caused that scar. He was clearly expecting her to follow him, and after a second's hesitation she did.

She didn't usually leave parties with perfect strangers. Despite her party-girl reputation, she wasn't quite the wild child her older sister Bella was. She didn't do one-night stands. She preferred to dance and laugh and flirt—and then go home alone.

Yet hadn't the rules changed? Hadn't *she* changed? She wasn't Zoe Balfour any more. She could do whatever she wanted. And she'd sensed in Max Monroe something she felt in herself, a darkness, a despair. Like called to like, she supposed, and she wanted to follow him.

She wanted to be with him.

Of course, there was no denying he was an attractive man. Her belly clenched, a coil of desire unfurling and spreading out through her limbs with sleepy warmth as she stared at his broad back and trim hips, his long, powerful legs still taking their careful strides as he weaved his way through the party's crowd, and Zoe followed. She wasn't, she realised belatedly as they made it to the foyer, even conscious of the stares.

She handed her ticket to the woman at the coat check and took her filmy wrap. Max, she saw, had uttered a few terse instructions into his mobile. He slid it back into his jacket pocket and turned to her.

'My car will be here in a moment.'

'Brilliant,' Zoe answered, for lack of anything else to say. She was realising how little she knew this man, how tense and even angry he seemed.

Was this—could this possibly be—a good idea?

'You don't have to come,' he said abruptly. Zoe started in surprise. 'You seem nervous.'

She gave a little shrug. 'No matter what you may think, this isn't my usual behaviour.'

'Oh?' He arched one eyebrow, his expression one of slightly smug curiosity. He had her all figured out, Zoe supposed. Or thought he did. Well, she'd thought she had herself figured out too. She was only now realising she didn't. 'So what is your normal behaviour?' He paused. 'Who are you?'

The question startled her, for it was the question she had not been wanting to ask herself for these past three weeks. She stared at him in astonished silence until he clarified impatiently, 'I just want your name.'

'Zoe.'

He arched his eyebrow a little higher. 'Just Zoe?'

'Yes,' she said firmly. 'Just Zoe.'

A limo pulled sleekly to the curb outside the gallery, and with one arm Max ushered her outside.

The air was balmy, the darkness soft around them. Zoe

glanced around, realising she was on a tiny side street in Soho
with no idea where or how to find a cab if she even wanted
one. The street was empty, the sidewalks deserted, and somewhere in the distance a car alarm set to a mournful wailing.

A man in a chauffeur's uniform jumped out of the driver's
seat and opened the limo's door, gesturing for Zoe to enter.

'Having second thoughts?' Max murmured in her ear.
His breath, cool and scented with mint and champagne,
tickled her cheek.

'More like third thoughts,' Zoe quipped, and a tiny smile
flickered across Max's face, easing the tension and lightening his features.

'You're a beautiful woman, Zoe,' he said. His face was
half averted to her, yet still he slowly, carefully reached out
to brush a tendril of hair away from her bare shoulder, his
cool fingers barely skimming her skin. She quivered under
the tiny caress. 'I'm sure any man in there would want to
be in my position right now.'

'Most assuredly,' she agreed lightly. Her heart had
started to hammer and she felt suddenly, unreasonably,
dizzy with longing. No single touch had ever affected her
so much. Made her want so much.

Made her forget…if only for a moment, for a night.

He reached out again, this time letting his fingers caress
her collarbone, barely brushing her skin, yet still making
her quiver and ache deep inside with an unexpected and
fierce longing. 'It's up to you, of course.'

Slowly Zoe nodded. When Max Monroe touched her,
every thought—every memory, every fear—went clean out
of her head. *That* was what she wanted.

Not just passion, but oblivion.

Slowly, silently, she climbed into the car.

Max climbed in after her, and the chauffeur closed the

door. Within seconds they were speeding through the night, the darkness relieved only by the passing lights of an occasional taxi.

Zoe sat back against the plush leather seat, surveying the well-stocked minibar and contemplated downing most of its contents. Had she really just climbed into a car with a total stranger? An angry, bitter, sardonic stranger at that? Well, she thought, swallowing a bubble of nervous laughter, at least it was a limo.

'Nice ride,' she said, and forced herself to relax—or at least seem relaxed—stretching her arms along the back of the seat, letting her head fall back as if she were utterly comfortable, completely in her element. 'So where are we going?'

Although Max sat next to her, he suddenly seemed oceans away, his face averted from hers as he stared out the window at the darkness.

'My apartment is in Tribeca. Unless you'd rather go somewhere else?' He turned to her, his smile—although it didn't quite *feel* like a smile—gleaming in the darkness.

'And miss seeing your place? I'm sure it's something fabulous.' She gave him a breezy smile and shook her hair back over her shoulders.

'And I'm sure you're quite used to fabulous,' he murmured, and she laughed, the sound husky.

'Absolutely.'

They didn't speak again, lapsing into a silence that was tense with unspoken thoughts. Expectations.

Zoe smoothed her silky black trousers, nervously pleating the fabric between her fingers before she forced herself to stop, and affected an air of unconcerned insouciance once more.

The limo came to a stop, and Zoe slipped out after Max. They were on a patch of old cobbled pavement—murder for her heels—in front of what looked like an abandoned warehouse near the waterfront. Zoe's heart lurched against her ribs. Oh, Lord, what had she got herself into? She turned around; the limo had disappeared and there wasn't a soul in sight…except Max.

He stood on the uneven cobbles, looking almost frozen, as if he didn't know where he was going, or was actually afraid to move.

The look of uncertainty on his face visible in the sickly yellow glare of a street lamp banished Zoe's own fears and compelled her to ask gently, 'Max…?'

'This way.' He spoke brusquely, shaking off that strange, uncertain look, the way a dog shakes off water, before striding across the sidewalk with long, deliberate steps to the warehouse.

Of course, Zoe saw as they approached the building, it wasn't an abandoned warehouse at all. Perhaps it once had been, but as they came closer signs of its upscale refurbishment were clearly visible. Instead of what had first looked like broken or blank windows, Zoe saw they were merely tinted. The front doors were made of the same thick, tinted glass, with polished chrome handles. A doorman leapt to attention as they approached and swung the doors open. Max stalked through them, in an almost military march, with Zoe hurrying behind in her heels.

This wasn't, she thought a bit resentfully, the most auspicious beginning to the evening. Yet even so, she wasn't tempted to turn away. Max Monroe fascinated her, and more than that, he somehow managed to reach a place inside of her she hadn't known existed, even now wasn't sure was real. When he'd touched her she felt something stir to life that she hadn't realised was asleep—or perhaps even dead. Something—someone—

that had nothing to do with Zoe Balfour, and all to do with just Zoe.

And that was why she followed him through the building's foyer with its polished floor of slick black marble, to the bank of gleaming, high-speed lifts. Max stepped inside, his finger trailing along the buttons until he reached the top one, and pushed *PH*. The penthouse. Of course.

The Balfour apartment on Park Avenue was a penthouse as well, with its dignified drawing rooms and separate servants' quarters. It was a beautiful, well-preserved relic from another age, a different century, and Zoe knew instinctively Max Monroe's penthouse was going to be something else entirely.

And it was. The lift doors opened straight into the apartment, and Zoe felt as if she were stepping into the sky. The apartment had floor-to-ceiling windows on every side, and the Hudson River gleamed only a block away, the lights of one of Manhattan's many bridges twinkling in the distance.

She turned, and from the other side saw the Empire State Building's needle point heavenward, a sea of skyscrapers behind it, filling the horizon.

She turned slowly in a full circle, savouring the view from every direction, until she finally chuckled a bit in admiration and turned to Max, who had shrugged out of his jacket and was even now loosening his tie. He didn't look at the view at all.

'Impressive,' she murmured. 'Do you ever grow tired of the view?'

'No.' He spoke so flatly Zoe wondered if she'd said something wrong.

Max moved around the apartment, flicking on a few lamps, bathing the room in a warm glow. Zoe glanced at the austere furnishings: all high-end bachelor pad with sleek leather sofas and uncomfortable-looking chairs made out of chrome, a designer glass coffee table she thought she'd seen featured in a decorating magazine, and a glimpse of a spotlessly clean stainless-steel kitchen that looked to have every gadget and appliance and was clearly never used.

Her heels clicked against the Brazilian cherry-wood floor as she came to stand by a window. Actually, Zoe saw, it was a door, made so seamlessly it looked like a window except for a discreet metal handle that led out to a wide terrace.

She heard Max cross the floor, felt him stand behind her. It amazed her how attuned she was to his movements, so that even before he reached out she knew he was going to touch her, was *waiting* for him to touch her.

He lifted his arm slowly—so slowly—and Zoe tensed, ready for his touch. Yet when it came it still shocked her, the heaviness of his hand on her bare shoulder sending ripples of awareness along her arm and through her body, deep into her belly. Neither of them spoke.

His hand slid along her shoulder, down her arm, as if he were slowly, languorously learning the landscape of her body. His fingers twined with hers as he pulled her around so she was facing him, his eyes dark and fathomless, his face seeming harsh in the yellow light cast from the buildings behind her, a sea of sightless skyscrapers. He moved so her back pressed against the glass and she could feel his heat, the hardness of his chest and thighs.

Her heart hammered with slow, deliberate thuds and her knees actually felt weak. She'd never had such a reaction to a man—to anyone, anything—before. And he hadn't even kissed her.

Yet he was going to, Zoe knew that, felt it. She wanted him to, and yet she could hardly believe this was happening, that she'd come here, found him. Her nerves leapt to life and she opened her mouth to say—what? Something, preferably something light or clever, to diffuse the intensity of the moment, of *him*, but before she uttered a word—and she wasn't even sure she *could*—she was prevented by his mouth coming down on hers.

His lips were hard, the kiss urgent and even a little angry, as if this moment was all either of them might ever have. His fingers slipped from hers, his hands sliding under her top to cup her breasts, and Zoe gasped at the sudden, intimate touch.

Her senses reeled; her body jerked into an instinctive and powerful response, and she found herself answering him kiss for kiss, the sorrow and despair of the past few weeks overflowing from her soul into this one caress. The intensity of Max's kiss, as well as her own response, surprised her—this wasn't even like her. She wasn't used to feeling this much, had been keeping it at bay these past weeks, maybe forever, and yet—

Yet she couldn't stop herself from responding, from her hands travelling up Max's hard, muscled shoulders to his hair—surprisingly soft—pulling him closer, as if she could take him right into her skin, fuse their bodies and melt into one.

It frightened her, this feeling so much. Wanting so much. From somewhere she summoned the strength to pull away—or try to, for she was trapped against the wall of glass. She arched her head back, her hair cascading down her back, so she could look at his face. Colour stained his cheekbones; his eyes were closed, his breathing ragged.

'In a hurry, are we?' she finally managed, but if she'd meant to sound light and unaffected, she failed. Her voice came out in little more than a gasp, and her body shook with the aftershocks of emotion.

He drew in a breath, and slid his hands from her breasts up to her shoulders, threading his fingers through her hair, his thumbs massaging her scalp. 'Why waste time?' he murmured.

'I'm sure you get plenty of women with that approach.' With the last of her willpower Zoe slipped under his arms, away from the cage of his body, and walked across the floor on legs that were far too wobbly.

Max propped one shoulder against the window, one hand in his trouser pocket. He looked remarkably recovered. Zoe felt as weak as a newborn kitten, a motherless lamb.

'You want to *talk*?' he asked with the slightest sneer, but it was still—considering what had just happened—enough to wound. Zoe sank into one of the chrome chairs—more comfortable than she'd expected—and arched an eyebrow.

'Silly me,' she said, and her voice finally sounded light and droll. 'I thought you might have mastered the art of conversation.'

'Only when necessary.' He walked slowly along the outside of the room, one hand trailing along the glass wall, so Zoe felt as if she were a powerless prey being circled by a hungry predator. He stopped in front of a chrome-and-glass drinks table; a bottle of whisky and a tumbler were already neatly laid out. He poured himself a finger's worth, his movements deliberate and precise. 'So,' he finally said, sipping his drink and swivelling to face her, 'you're from England.'

'Yes.'

'Just visiting, or do you live here?'

Zoe hesitated. 'Visiting,' she said finally. 'For now.'

'No firm plans?' Again, that slight sneer that still hurt. More than it should.

She smiled with a breezy confidence she was far from feeling. Seemingly innocent questions, yet each one possessed its own little sting. 'No. Never. I'm not that kind of girl.'

'Ah.'

'And what about you?'

He took another sip of his drink. 'What about me?'

'You're a businessman.'

'Yes.'

'What do you do, exactly?'

'Business.'

Zoe rolled her eyes. 'How enlightening.'

'I manage investments. I buy companies. I take risks.' He shrugged, the movement one of powerful, eloquent dismissal. 'I make money.'

'Money is good.'

His mouth quirked up in something that looked like a smile but didn't feel like one. 'Isn't it just.'

'How did you get that scar?' The question popped out inadvertently; she hadn't meant to ask it. She suspected he was sensitive about it, perhaps self-conscious. And how could he not be? It was noticeable, impossible to ignore, a livid line of whitened flesh from his eyebrow to his chin, snaking along the side of his nose, a vivid reminder of—what? Something, he'd said. Something terrible.

'An accident.' He spoke flatly, unemotionally, yet Zoe sensed the darkness—the sorrow and despair and even the fury—pulsing underneath. He said the word *accident* the way she said *illegitimate*.

'It must have been some accident.'

'It was.'

'Were you alone?'

'Yes.' He paused, his throat working before he elaborated in that same flat tone. 'I was flying my plane.'

'You're a pilot?'

'I was.' He paused. 'Recreationally.'

His voice was flat, his face expressionless as he took a sip of his drink.

'So.' Zoe tried to keep her voice light, as if her tone could stave off the darkness emanating from Max, swirling around her soul. 'What happened?'

'I crashed.' He smiled, the curve of his mouth terribly cold. 'It happens.'

'I suppose so.' Zoe crossed and recrossed her legs, searching for something to say. 'You're lucky you escaped with your life,' she finally said, and at that moment it felt like a terribly inane sentiment.

'Oh, yes,' Max agreed, and there was a darker note in his voice now, the pulsing emotion underneath bubbling to the fore, as hot and dangerous—and fascinating—as a latent volcano. He walked towards her with slow, deliberate strides. 'I'm very lucky.'

Zoe resisted the urge to press back against the chair. She didn't like the dark look in Max's eyes, the sudden, cruel twist of the mouth she'd just kissed.

'How long have you been flying?' she asked in a desperate attempt to restore a sense of normality to the moment. It didn't work; Max just kept walking. He stopped only when he was a hand span away, and then, to her surprise, he dropped to his knees in front of her so they were level, his eyes gazing darkly, intently, intensely, into hers.

They stared at each other for a moment, neither speaking, the only sound the harsh tear of their breathing. Zoe felt trapped, transfixed, and yet with a strange, new need inside her. What was happening here?

Max didn't move, didn't tear his gaze from hers—it was as if he were waiting, needing something…needing her…

Then, out of instinct and even her own need, Zoe

reached out—with the same careful deliberation he had touched her moments ago—and with the tip of one finger traced the jagged path of the scar along his face. The damaged flesh was surprisingly smooth, almost silky, and faintly puckered.

Zoe didn't know why she did it, didn't know how Max would react. She didn't really know what was happening here, what this feeling was between them—so much *feeling*. Pain and sorrow and even a jagged little shard of hope.

Max stilled, tensing under her touch, and then she felt him relax, the resistance trickling from his body, leaving him loose and pliant under her hand. He closed his eyes. Her finger rested on the edge of the scar by his chin; she could feel his stubble. Then, still acting out of instinct and an even deeper desire, Zoe leant forward and kissed that wounded place, her lips lingering on his skin as she breathed in his scent, mint and musk.

Max shuddered.

Zoe drew back, strangely shaken, and her gaze flew to Max's face. He'd opened his eyes and was staring at her with a blatant hunger that both thrilled and alarmed her. He reached forward and cupped her face in his hands, his fingers sliding along her cheekbones, and he drew her to him so their lips barely touched.

He brushed his lips against hers once, and then again, and then kissed her with a gentleness that was so different from that first angry encounter. It made Zoe's insides sweetly melt, until a deeper, rawer urgency made her deepen that little kiss, and her hands came up to grip Max's shoulders.

She didn't know how long they remained that way, only knew the glorious sweetness of a kiss so deep and unending it felt as if they were exploring each other's souls. Then Max scooped her up in his arms; she felt as tiny and treasured as a doll, nestled against his chest, curling into him with a surprising naturalness. He carried her with the careful, deliberate strides she was becoming accustomed to into the bedroom.

Like the living room, the bedroom was all windows, and light from the buildings outside filtered through the venetian blinds, bathing the room in luminescence. Max set her down on a huge bed, the navy satin sheets slippery under her. She looked up at him; his expression was shuttered and yet grave. She waited.

Slowly Max brushed a tendril of hair away from her face, his fingers skimming her cheek, her eyebrow, the ridge of her nose. Then he dropped his hand and began to unbutton his shirt.

Zoe watched, unable to keep her gaze from the expanse of broad, muscled chest revealed by the gap in his shirt; she reached out and helped him shrug the garment off, letting her fingers trail his skin as his had hers, enjoying the feel of hard muscle, crisp hair.

Still, neither of them spoke, and Zoe wondered if it was because they had no need of words, or because they were afraid words might break this moment, shatter the precious, fragile bond that had silently sprung and stretched between them.

The only sound was the whisper and slither of clothes as they undressed each other, the slide of silk to the floor as Zoe shrugged out of her halter top and trousers. Then they lay naked on the satin sheets, staring at each other for a long moment. Zoe wanted to speak, to say something, and the words clogged in her throat, too many words. She wanted to tell Max she might not have a scar on her face, but there was one on her soul. She wanted to explain that, like him, she'd had an accident—an accident of birth. And, she suspected, like him, it had left her wrecked and wondering how to rebuild a life that had been virtually destroyed, if there even *was* a life to rebuild.

Yet she said none of it, despite the pressure building inside her, in her chest and behind her eyes. She blinked away the sting of tears she hadn't expected and when Max kissed her again, his hands skimming her body, learning all of its curves and dips and secret places, she gave herself up to the sweet oblivion and let the words—and the thoughts, the fears—trickle away...at least for now.

Afterwards Max lay on his back, Zoe resting in the curve of his arm, her slender body curled towards the shelter of his. A tendril of her hair tickled his nose, and he breathed in that now-familiar scent of rose water. Shampoo, he surmised, and smiled.

He wasn't used to smiling, not a real smile anyway, and he wasn't accustomed to feeling this good. His body hummed with sleepy satiation, his limbs languid and heavy, and he felt, for the moment, utterly replete.

How strange.

For weeks—since that moment on the plane when his world had gone totally, terrifyingly black—he'd felt as if he were missing something. Losing something, bit by bit, so his body and his soul and his tormented mind all hungered for it, cried out for it.

Yet now, amazingly, he felt as if he'd been given something. He felt full. Blessed, even.

Ridiculous.

He heard Zoe give a little sigh and knew she was asleep; her head was heavy on his arm. He had no intention of sleeping himself, no desire to surrender to the weakness of dreams, or have Zoe see him in such a humiliatingly vulnerable state.

Carefully he extracted himself and rolled to a sitting position, his feet flat on the floor. The clothes were scattered haphazardly, and it took a moment for him to find his boxers. He pulled them on and then oriented himself by the foot of the bed; it was six steps to the door to the terrace.

Outside, the air had turned chilly and damp, and a breeze blew over him, cooling his heated skin. Ten steps to the railing; in the darkness he could make out very little, and he made a note to have all the terrace furniture removed. He'd hardly need it, as he doubted he'd spend much time out here.

Do you ever grow tired of the view?

No, he never had. He'd lost it before he had the chance.

Max closed his eyes. *Stop feeling sorry for yourself.* He didn't know if the voice inside his head was his own or his father's. No point in whining, regretting. Just get on with it. Get on with living.

Yet this didn't feel like living. This, he acknowledged starkly, felt like slowly dying. Yet even as this realization dawned, another followed closely on its heels.

What had happened in there, with Zoe—just Zoe— hadn't felt like dying. That had been life in its purest, most elemental form. He'd never experienced a night like that with a woman before, and he'd had plenty of nights. Plenty of women. Yet never had he felt so attuned with another person before, moving truly as one flesh.

Or was he just romanticising a tawdry encounter, imbuing it with more meaning that it actually had because he knew he would not have another night like it? He couldn't hide his encroaching blindness forever, couldn't keep the darkness at bay. The doctor had given him months, perhaps only weeks. Perhaps, Max thought as he struggled to identify the Chrysler Tower amidst the blurred shapes of the Manhattan skyline, only days.

And then what? What could his future possibly look like, what shape could it take?

He had no idea, couldn't imagine the suffocating darkness all the time, endlessly blindfolded. Just the thought of it made his chest hurt as he fought back the encroaching panic. At least now he had some visibility, some light. Some sanity.

He turned away from the view he couldn't really see. He would allow Zoe to sleep until morning, and then she would have to go. There was no point in her staying. Not that she would even want to stay; it had been clear to both of them what this night was...simply that, a night.

He took ten steps to the door, another six to the bed. From the light outside he could see the golden halo of her hair spread on the pillow, the pale, bare shoulder above the ink-coloured sheet.

She was a shallow, spoiled socialite. Every indication proved that assessment true. No matter what she had said, nights like these were simply par for the course. So why did the thought of her walking away in the morning feel like a punch straight to the gut?

To the heart?

Gently, so gently she didn't even stir, he slid his hand along her shoulder, across her cheek, feeling—seeing—her for the last time. His hand stilled as his thumb brushed moisture clinging to her lashes.

A tear?

Why would a woman like her—a spoiled socialite—be crying?

Regret and guilt bit at him. He knew he was dismissing her; he knew he needed to.

To believe she was more, could be more to him, was both dangerous and pointless.

They had no future together.

They couldn't.

Max let his hand fall away and stretched out next to her, making sure not to brush against the inviting warmth of her body. He lay there, staring sightlessly ahead, waiting for sleep to come. He both hated and craved sleep, for while it granted oblivion, it also meant darkness and dreams.

More darkness.

CHAPTER THREE

ZOE woke slowly to sunlight, felt it stream over her sheet-covered body and warm her face. She kept her eyes closed, enjoying the warmth as she stretched slowly, languorously, the satin sheet cool against her bare skin.

She was naked.

In an instant the memories rushed back, tumbling through her mind, making her smile. Her body still hummed with satisfaction; her heart felt full.

Last night… Last night had been wonderful.

She opened her eyes; sunlight streamed in from the wall of windows, bathing the room in cheerful morning light, slanting golden shafts across the empty bed.

Max was gone.

Zoe was surprised it had taken her this long to realise it; his absence was enormous, as if there was a great jagged hole next to her instead of an empty expanse of navy satin. Slowly she pulled the sheet around her, tucking it firmly across her breasts. Still, it trailed across the floor, and as she stepped over her scattered garments from last night she almost considered pulling them on, but then couldn't bear to do such a thing, for somehow—unreasonably perhaps—it relegated last night to something tawdry and temporary, and she didn't think it was.

Hoped it wasn't.

Was she simply being naive?

Last night she'd wanted to forget who she was, what she was, in Max's arms. She had, and amazingly, she'd woken feeling new. Different.

In Max's arms she'd felt whole. Healed.

Loved.

Now she realised she was being ridiculous. She barely knew the man; he certainly didn't know her, *just* Zoe. Could one night—one amazing night—really change that?

Zoe slipped into the living room, the morning light making the room seem all the more sparely chic and austere. And empty. Max wasn't there. She looked in the kitchen, peeked in two other bedrooms, a study, a library and a dining room with a table that looked able to seat twenty—but probably never sat a soul—and couldn't find him anywhere.

Had he actually *left*?

She stood in the middle of the library with its walls lined with leather-bound books, a huge mahogany desk in one corner. A scent of leather and pipe tobacco hung faintly in the air, and for a moment Zoe was reminded with painful force of home, of her father.

Oscar.

Uncertainty—and fear—gnawed at her.

She gazed around, the sheet slipping slightly, pooling in inky satin around her feet, and then she saw him.

Of course, he was outside. She'd glanced out at the terrace when she'd first entered the living room and hadn't seen him, but now she saw it wrapped around the entire apartment, and he was on the other side, through the dining room.

She crossed the two rooms, the sheet trailing behind her in a dark river, and opened the doors that led out to the terrace.

'There you are.' She spoke lightly, but still she heard—
and felt—the uncertain wobble in her tone. Felt the flutter
of fear in her heart. Max was seated at a wrought-iron
table, a thick ceramic mug of coffee cradled between his
palms. He looked lost in thought, and he glanced up only
as she came to stand near him, feeling a bit ridiculous
wrapped in a sheet.

Why on earth hadn't she put her clothes on?

'Here I am,' he agreed, and Zoe couldn't tell a thing
from his tone.

'Did you make coffee?' she asked, making sure to keep
her voice light. 'I didn't smell any in the kitchen, but I'm
gasping for a—'

'I made it hours ago. It's cold.' Now she was able to recognise his tone, and it was frighteningly flat.

'Oh.' She paused, hitching the sheet more firmly around
her. 'Well, perhaps I could make another pot. And maybe
borrow one of your shirts?' She raised her eyebrows,
tossing her hair over her shoulders, determined to seem far
more insouciant and confident than she felt. What man
could resist a woman wrapped in a sheet after all?

'I don't think that's a good idea.'

Apparently Max could. Zoe's hand clenched on the sheet,
and the satin slipped under her fingers. Max regarded her with
a remote coolness that made her throat dry and her eyes sting.

No. No, please, no. Not this. Not this utter rejection, the
look in his eyes one of…annoyance? Zoe feared that was the
humiliating emotion she saw there. She was no more than
an irritation to be dealt with before he got on with his day.

Or was she overreacting? Battle scarred from all the
trashy tabloid talk, the stares and whispers?

'Why?' she finally asked, and forced herself to smile.
'Are you out of coffee?'

'No, I'm not,' Max replied. 'But I don't think you should stay long enough to warrant coffee or clothes.'

Zoe blinked. She felt as if she'd been slapped. She opened her mouth but for once any witty retort or rejoinder deserted her. Her mind was blank, numb, and she looked away, blinking hard.

'I can't say much for your hospitality,' she finally managed. Her voice sounded scratchy, and her throat felt sore.

'No,' Max agreed. His mouth was set in a hard line, the expression in his eyes chilly and so terribly resolute.

'Did last night not mean anything to you?' Zoe asked, wincing even as the words came out of her mouth. What a stupid question to ask. Obviously it didn't; he really couldn't make it any plainer. Was she a glutton for punishment, demanding the torture of him explaining himself even more?

'No,' Max said again, and Zoe bit her lip. 'And I don't think it meant much to you either.'

How could he say that, Zoe wondered, when she'd felt so different, so *new*? How could he believe it? Pride forced herself to smile coolly and toss her hair over her shoulders. 'Well, even so, a parting cup of coffee would be a courtesy, at least.'

'Sorry.' He didn't sound sorry at all.

'Right. Well.' She gripped the sheet tightly; the last thing she wanted was for the thing to fall off completely and leave her standing completely naked in front of this man who had used and rejected her with a clinical, cold cruelty.

And she had let him.

She'd wanted to forget…and she had to give Max that— he'd allowed her to forget.

And now she just had more pain and heartache to remember. To try to forget…again.

'You might want to explain to your future lovers that you have a strict morning-after policy,' she said, gripping a handful of sheet, her teeth gritted even though she managed to keep her voice cutting rather than wobbly, as if she were angry rather than desolate or even heartbroken. 'Out before eight o'clock.'

'Actually, it's almost nine,' Max drawled in a bored voice. 'But I'll keep that in mind.'

'Bastard,' Zoe hissed. She couldn't keep herself from saying it; it was better than crying.

Max swivelled to face her fully for the first time since she'd come out on the terrace.

'You knew what you were getting into, Zoe,' he said coolly. '*Just* Zoe. Some men might sugarcoat it a bit more than I do, but the fact remains the same. We had a night together, and it's over. Now I have work to do.'

He rose from his chair, one hand braced against the table. Zoe didn't move, and his mouth tightened.

'You need to go.'

'What about—' Zoe swallowed the words. What was the point of asking, *What about when I touched your scar? I held you in my arms. It felt like so much more. It meant so much more…to me.*

She was so very, very stupid.

'Fine.'

In a whirl of satin she stalked from the terrace, and it was a testament to her rage that she didn't even care when the sheet caught in the door and came undone, leaving her utterly bare.

Naked she strode through the rooms, too angry to care— or at least to acknowledge she cared—and found her clothes in the bedroom. She jerked them on, reaching for her wrap and handbag by the door before she stabbed viciously at the lift button.

It seemed an age before the elevator finally arrived, and she stood there, taut, her chest heaving with the effort of containing her emotion, unable to turn and look at—for—Max, to see the scorn that would undoubtedly be twisting his features. Finally the doors opened, signalling her freedom, her exile. She could feel Max behind her, even though she hadn't looked at him once since he'd told her to go.

Now as she stepped into the lift she whirled around, determined to give him one parting shot.

'Go to he—' The words, ripped from her, were cut off as she gazed at him still standing by the door to the terrace, the sheet she'd worn pressed to his face, his eyes closed.

He didn't seem aware of her at all, and before she could say—or think—anything more, the doors whooshed closed and she was speeding down, away from Max Monroe forever.

The sheet smelled ever so faintly of rose water. Max breathed it in, his eyes still closed, trying to reconstruct her face, the feel of her body, in his mind. A memory.

Everything was becoming a memory.

Sighing, the sound harsh with regret, he dropped the sheet. He'd almost tripped over the blasted thing, and he'd only meant to kick it away, but when he'd smelled that faint, lingering scent…

He sighed again, and then he cursed.

It was over. He'd never see Zoe again. He let out a sharp laugh at the irony of his words. Of course he'd never *see* Zoe again. That was why he'd sent her away as callously as he had. Admittedly he'd never spent more than a few days— sometimes weeks—with a woman, but he favoured them with more dignity and respect than he'd just treated Zoe.

He'd had no choice. The cut had to be clean. Sharp. Final.

Everything felt so final.

Cursing again, Max walked with careful steps to the study. At least he had his work… for now. When would that be taken from him? How could he consult or invest when he couldn't even read a newspaper or a computer screen? Already those tasks were proving difficult, near impossible, and it was only a matter of time before everything went blank. Black.

Forever.

And he was left powerless, as helpless as a child once more. He couldn't bear to feel that again, and he certainly couldn't bear for anyone to see him like that.

That was why he'd sent Zoe away.

Bastard.

Yes, he was a bastard, and she was a shallow socialite, and they'd forget each other in a fortnight. For his own sake, Max prayed that were true.

Go to hell.

Max smiled grimly. He was already there.

Zoe took a taxi back to the Balfour apartment, barely conscious of the blocks speeding by, a blur of traffic lights. Her body and mind both ached, and she felt utterly exhausted. Spent.

Used.

She gritted her teeth, trying to keep Max's words—his sneer—at bay. *Some men might sugarcoat it a bit more than I do…*

That was an understatement.

Sighing she leant her head against the windowpane of the cab. The morning sunshine had given way to grey, and outside a light drizzle fell, misting over Grand Central Station. The weather matched her mood perfectly.

Why had she gone with Max last night? What had she been hoping to achieve? Even though she liked a party, she was choosy with her partners. She didn't hop into bed with just anyone, and yet last night...

Last night had been different. Max had been different.

Or so she'd thought. She winced, remembering that feeling of glorious optimism she'd felt when she'd woken in a pool of sunshine in Max's bed. She'd felt as if it was the beginning; she thought she'd finally found herself.

Hardly.

Nothing had changed; she hadn't changed. Max Monroe was a self-serving ass and she was just what she'd been before, and what she'd called him—a bastard.

The apartment was dark and quiet when Zoe entered, flinging her keys on the marble table in the grand entrance foyer. Oscar Balfour hired a full-time housekeeper to maintain the apartment, but she had weekends off and Zoe was glad. She wanted to be alone. She needed to be alone; she didn't think she could handle a conversation of any kind at this point.

She stripped off her clothes, kicking them into a corner, vowing never to wear them again. Then she strode into the marble en-suite bathroom and ran a full, foaming tub, hot enough to almost hurt, sinking into the bubbles in blessed relief.

She stayed in the water until her fingers and toes looked like prunes, and it had gone from steaming to tepid to cold. Only then did she reluctantly rouse herself from the blank state of lethargy she'd snuggled into like a cocoon, blocking out the world and its harsh judgements and memories. She put on the pair of pyjamas no one ever saw her in—an old pair of grey track bottoms and a worn-to-softness hoody—and curled up in bed, her knees to her chest.

All around her the apartment was quiet, dark. Empty. Curled on the huge bed, she'd never felt more alone. More lonely. Spinning in a great, empty void of uncertainty and uselessness.

And then before she could stop herself, the tears she'd been holding back for not just hours but weeks came rushing down her face, scalding her cheeks, emptying her soul.

She didn't know how long she cried, the sobs racking her body as for once she didn't hold anything back, didn't pretend even to herself that she was all right, that she was strong as her father had told her she was.

She wasn't. She wasn't, Zoe thought as she wiped her cheeks, anything at all. The loss of the Balfour name had been the loss of her identity. It was humiliating to realise that, to feel as though she had nothing to call her own, nothing to *be*.

And had she actually thought—if only for a few hours— that Max Monroe could give that to her? That with him she'd know who she was?

'I know who I am,' Zoe said aloud. Her voice sounded small and forlorn, pathetic. Yet still hugging her knees to her chest, she reminded herself of just what kind of woman she was. What she could do best.

Sparkle.

And so she would.

She sparkled and partied and kept herself busy, all of her energy and emotion poured into the trivial matters of shopping sample sales and deciding what the best entertainment for an evening was. She came back to the apartment only to deposit her shopping bags and to sleep, and she determinedly ignored the housekeeper Lila's silent censure.

She refused to think about Max. She didn't think about anything, anyone, not even herself. Yet with each party she

felt herself becoming more fragile, more frantic, clinging
to a way of life that was surely slipping out of her grasp.
Perhaps it had been for years, and it took the outing of her
birth to make her realise she couldn't be an it-girl forever.
Eventually you had to grow up. You had to do something.

You had to be strong.

Except she had no idea how to be strong, or even who
she was, or how to go about finding out.

Three weeks after her night with Max, Oscar called her.
Zoe wouldn't have even answered—she didn't want to talk
to her so-called father—but she'd been asleep and she
reached for her mobile in a half-stupor.

'Zoe?' Oscar's sharp tone had her scrambling to a
sitting position.

'Dadd—' She pressed her lips together, and heard
Oscar sigh.

'I hadn't heard from you since you arrived in New York,
Zoe, and I wanted to make sure you were all right. You
sound as if you were asleep—'

'I was.'

'It's one o'clock in the afternoon.'

'I was out late last night.'

The tiny, arctic pause told Zoe Oscar wasn't happy
about that. 'Am I to understand you have not taken steps
to reach your father?'

'He's not my father.'

'Indeed.' Oscar's tone gentled. 'But you know who I am
talking about, Zoe, and—'

'I haven't decided if I want to find him,' Zoe cut him off.
'I'm not sure what good it will do. He hasn't been interested in me before now—'

'I doubt he knew of your existence.'

'You don't think my mother ever told him?' The

question came out stilted. *My mother.* Who was she? Bella
and Olivia had memories; she had nothing but the knowledge that she was the cause of her mother's death. The only
mother she had really ever known had been Oscar's third
wife, Lillian, and she'd died months ago. The loss was still
fresh, painful, leaving her feeling even more adrift.

'I doubt it, Zoe.' Oscar paused. 'But even if she did,
his position was hardly tenable. She was married, you
know, to me.'

'Well, still,' Zoe said, hearing a petulant note creep into
her voice. 'I don't know if I want to find him.'

'Then perhaps you should return here,' Oscar said after
a moment, 'to Balfour Manor.'

Balfour Manor…the only place she'd ever really thought
of as home, with its gracious rooms and rolling lawns, its
sense of history and honour, certain of its dignified place
in the world.

If only she felt the same.

'Zoe…?' Oscar prompted, and she shook her head even
though he couldn't see her.

'I can't.' She couldn't face everyone's pity or curiosity,
the tabloids who wouldn't let go of her story, or the fair-
weather friends who would turn—already had—at the first
sign of rain. She couldn't, even though part of her—a large
part—longed to flee back to the safe haven of home.

'If you can't go back,' Oscar told her, a smile in his
voice, 'then go forward. That's why you're in New York—
not just to ring up the charges on my credit card.' Although
the kindness in his tone took the sting out of the words, Zoe
still flushed guiltily.

'OK,' she finally said, the one word given reluctantly,
and Oscar gave a tiny sigh.

'I love you, Zoe.'

Tears stung her eyes. She thought she'd cried them all already, yet there they were again, ready to fall. She blinked them back.

'I love you too,' she mumbled.

After she hung up the phone she clambered out of the bed and walked through the quiet, empty rooms of the Balfour apartment. Out on the penthouse's terrace, Zoe sank into a wrought-iron chair, drawing her legs up to her chest.

It was a gorgeous day, the sky a pale, washed blue, the trees in Central Park a vivid green. Even in the city everything smelled fresh, new.

If you can't go back, then go forward.

The thought terrified her. She had no idea what forward looked like, felt like. What it could mean.

Yet she knew of only one step forward to take, the step she'd been sent to New York for.

She needed to find her father.

CHAPTER FOUR

Zoe tilted her head back to survey the gleaming glass sky-scraper once more; it was one of the tallest, most imposing buildings on Fifty-Seventh Street. A brass plaque by the front doors, guarded by an official-looking doorman in a navy suit with gold braid, had two discreet words: *Anderson Finance*.

Thomas Anderson, the CEO and founder of the company, was the man she'd come to meet. Taking a deep breath, her nerves still jarring and jangling, she walked briskly into the building's foyer, favouring the doorman with an imperious nod, her heels clicking on the black marble floor.

'May I help you, miss?' A woman with an upswept do and a good deal of glossy make-up gave her a smile of official courtesy when Zoe was halfway to the bank of gleaming gold lifts.

She gave the woman a breezy smile. 'I'm here to see Thomas Anderson.'

The woman didn't even blink. 'Is he expecting you?' she asked, and Zoe gave her practised little trill of laughter.

'No, actually, it's a surprise.' She batted her eyelashes, and saw a brief look of distaste flicker across the woman's expertly made-up features.

'I'm afraid Mr Anderson doesn't like surprises,' the woman told her with a frosty smile. 'And he has back-to-back meetings all morning—'

'Then call up,' Zoe interjected. She smiled sweetly, even though her insides felt far too wobbly. 'Tell him…' She took a deep breath. 'Tell him Zoe Balfour is here to see him.' Another breath. 'Alexandra Balfour's daughter.'

The woman pursed her lips and then reached for the phone. Zoe couldn't hear what she said into that gleaming black receiver; her heart was beating so fast and loud it thundered in her ears. It took all of her strength to simply stand upright, a cool little smile on her face, looking for the world like the outcome of that ten-second phone call held no import whatsoever.

The woman put the receiver down and gave her a rather narrow look. 'He'll see you. Twenty-sixth floor.'

Zoe let her smile widen as she waggled her fingers and then she turned and walked crisply to the elevators, the click of her heels echoing all around her.

Her heart was still thudding right out of her chest and her finger trembled as she pushed twenty-six and then watched as each floor zoomed by, a reverse countdown.

A little ping announced she had arrived, and the elevator doors opened straight into a large reception room, endless yards of plush cream carpet scattered with leather sofas, a lot of modern art on the walls. Zoe glanced at a few blobs of colour daubed on a canvas and thought of Max's words to her at the gallery opening: *my company donated a quarter of a million dollars to fund these monstrosities on the walls*.

She smiled slightly, even though the memory of him still hurt, hurt more than it ever should, considering how little they really knew each other. Had known. Max Monroe was in the past; there would be no opportunities to know him more, or at all, in the future. She would do well to remember that.

A black-suited PA rose from behind a streamlined glass-topped desk and walked over to her. 'Zoe Balfour?'

'Yes.'

'Mr Anderson will see you now. I'm afraid he only has a few moments. He's got—'

'Back-to-back meetings,' Zoe filled in. 'So I heard.'

The PA threw her a startled look and Zoe realised how terse she sounded. She forced herself to smile.

The PA tapped on a pair of double doors of burnished mahogany before throwing them open and ushering Zoe into an office as huge and sleekly decorated as the waiting room. At the end of what seemed an acre of plush carpet a man waited behind a desk, his back to her. He gazed out the floor-to-ceiling windows of tinted glass at the bustling street below, a forest of skyscrapers stretching to the horizon.

Zoe recognised him from the photo she had, a grainy shot featured in the business section of the *New York Times*. His thick mane of salt-and-pepper hair, the wide set of his shoulders—she didn't even need to see his face to know this was the man she'd been looking for.

This was Thomas Anderson.

Her father.

Still, she wasn't prepared for the lightning bolt of shock that sliced through her when he finally turned, and she gazed into a pair of eyes as jade green as her own. She'd always felt like an anomaly among her sisters, with their dazzling Balfour blue eyes, the same as their father's. Hers were so different, and now she knew where those eyes came from, who had given them to her. And they were gazing at her now with an expression of cold courtesy.

'Miss Balfour? How may I help?'

He had no idea why she was here, Zoe thought numbly. Or at least he was good at pretending he didn't.

'I believe you knew my mother, Mr Anderson. Alexandra Balfour?'

He stilled, the expression in his eyes turning wary before it quickly cleared. 'I don't— Yes, a long time ago. I had business in London one summer and I believe we may have met.' He raised his eyebrows. 'Pardon me, Miss Balfour. I'd assumed you came here to ask on behalf of a charity or some such. I have numerous such requests and—'

'That's not why I came.' Zoe spoke through stiff lips. Not unless *she* was considered a charity. 'And you know it.' She didn't know where she found the courage or the conviction to say the last, but she knew it deep in her bones. Thomas Anderson knew exactly why she'd come here. He had to at least suspect. 'I expect, being in finance,' she continued coolly, 'you're rather good at maths.' He shrugged, and Zoe continued. 'It will be twenty-seven years ago this June that you met my mother.' She paused, watching him. 'I turned twenty-six in April.'

The silence was electric and went on for too long. Thomas Anderson's gaze had turned terribly cold. 'I'm afraid, Miss Balfour, I have no idea what you're talking about.'

Zoe stared at him, not wanting to feel the well of disappointed hope opening up inside of her, consuming her. Had she actually thought he might accept she was his daughter? Open his arms and embrace her like some prodigal child? And would she have even wanted that?

At least a small, desperate part of her would have. She recognised that by the disappointment and despair swamping her now. Her nails dug into her palms and she lifted her chin. 'I don't know how much of it reached the papers over here, Mr Anderson, but a little over a month

ago a story broke at the Balfour Charity Ball—a scandal.'
She paused; her father's expression didn't change. 'The
story was that my mother—Alexandra Balfour—had an
affair twenty-seven years ago, and her youngest daughter
was actually illegitimate.'

The smile he gave her was chilly. 'I'm afraid I don't read
the kinds of papers that run those stories, Miss Balfour.'

'No, you just live them.' The vitriol in her words
shocked both of them, but Zoe didn't apologise. 'This
episode of my mother's life was discovered in an old
journal she kept. She named you as my father.' There. It
was said. It wasn't exactly true—she hadn't written his
name—but how many American businessmen spent a
summer in London, had been invited to Balfour Manor and
had eyes the colour of jade?

Thomas Anderson stared at her for a long moment, and
for a second—no more—Zoe thought he would admit it.
Explain. Apologise. She longed for it, for the explanation
and, more importantly, the acceptance. Then she saw a
flicker of regret pass across his face like a shadow and he
turned away from her, back to the windows.

'I'm sorry,' he said quietly. 'I have no idea what you're
talking about.'

'Are you saying you didn't have an affair with my
mother?' Zoe demanded in both disbelief and despair.

He paused, a tiny hesitation but telling nonetheless. 'I
knew your mother socially, for a very brief time.'

'So she lied?' Zoe said, her voice turning raw. 'In a
journal she hid in a children's book, a journal she never
expected anyone to see, she lied?'

'I'm sorry,' Thomas said again. His back was to her, and
his voice was low.

'Just what are you sorry for?' Zoe demanded. 'Father-

ing me or not being able to admit it now? I could have a
DNA test done—'

'That would involve a court battle,' he returned sharply.
'I don't think either of us want to go there.'

More scandal. More shame. 'Why don't you want to
admit it?' Zoe whispered. She felt the sting of tears behind
her lids and she blinked hard. 'We have the same coloured
eyes,' she added in a choked voice. 'No one in my family—
no Balfour—has eyes that are green like mine. But you do.'

She saw his body tense and when he turned to her any
possible trace of compassion or pity had completely
vanished. He reached to press a button on his telephone.
'My security guard, Hans, will escort you out, Miss
Balfour. I believe our conversation is finished.' He paused,
his eyes—so green and so cold—meeting hers. 'I don't
think I need to warn you that if this story spreads somehow,
I could sue for slander.'

Zoe's eyes widened. 'You're threatening me?'

'Just stating a fact.'

She shook her head, her gaze falling on a large sterling-
silver picture frame on the desk. Slowly, numbly, she
reached over and turned it so she could see the photograph
inside. It was a picture of a family.

A woman in her early fifties perhaps, with a stylish bob
of silvery hair, and two boys and a girl. The girl, she saw
with a terrible, creeping numbness, was actually a woman,
about her own age. The boys were younger, perhaps in
their teens.

He had a family. Of course. She stood there, gazing at
her half-brothers and half-sister who would never know
her, who would never want to know her. She didn't belong
with them. She didn't belong with the Balfours.

She didn't belong anywhere.

Behind her the doors opened, and she felt a firm hand on her elbow. 'Miss Balfour, let me show you out,' a man said, his voice polite but unyielding.

Zoe shook off his arm. 'Don't touch me.' She turned back to Thomas Anderson, who was looking at her as if she were a bug he had just neatly squashed, a mixture of distaste and relief. 'You can deny it all you want,' she choked, 'but you and I both know the truth.' Hans grabbed her arm again, leading her backwards. Zoe gazed at her father, hurt and hatred boiling up within her and firing her words. 'We both know,' she said, 'and I'll never, ever forget this. Never.' The last word ended on a sob and, shaking off Hans once more, she turned around and strode from the room.

She wasn't aware of the curious gaze of her father's PA, or the several businessmen who entered the elevator on various floors as they sped down to the lobby. She ignored the woman at the front desk and the security guard who opened the door.

She could feel nothing but her own pain, see nothing but the look of utter rejection on her father's face. It was her deepest fear, her worst nightmare, and she'd just lived it.

Her head felt light and her vision swam; she tasted bile. She needed to find some composure, some control, but she couldn't even begin to know how. She took a deep breath, and another, trying to steady herself, but her stomach heaved and she bent over double, cold sweat prickling on her forehead.

From her handbag she heard the persistent trill of her mobile and with a wild, impossible lurch of hope she wondered if it was her father ringing, having second thoughts, wanting to apologise.

It was Karen. 'Zoe! I just wanted to make sure you're coming out with us tonight. There's a new club opening in the Village—'

Zoe leant against the side of the building and closed her eyes. Cold sweat still prickled on her forehead and her mouth tasted metallic. 'Is there?' she said dully. She could barely even make sense of Karen's words.

'Yes, of course there is! You sound a bit funny.' Karen sounded torn between impatience and concern. 'Are you all right?'

Zoe leant her head back against the brick wall. For an insane moment she wanted to confide just how not all right she was. *No, I'm not all right. I've been rejected outright by two men—maybe even two of the most important men in my life—in the space of two weeks. I don't know who I am or what I want to be, and I know I should have figured that out by now. I'm so scared.*

'I'm fine.' Karen wasn't the kind of friend who wanted to hear about those fears. She didn't have that kind of friend.

'So are you coming tonight?'

Zoe opened her eyes. 'Yes.'

She went out to the club with Karen and a bunch of New York friends determined to forget Thomas Anderson and Max Monroe. Both men—and their almost identical looks of sneering indifference—haunted her, their cold words of denial and rejection replaying in her mind, echoing through her heart. Still, Zoe tried to make a good show of it, dancing and laughing and flirting even though she felt so brittle inside, ready to break. After only an hour the club's pounding music made her head throb, and the cocktail she'd been drinking tasted sour. She left it virtually untouched on the bar and went in search of the loo.

The harsh lights in the ladies' put her own pale face into awful relief. She looked terrible, Zoe thought rather distantly as she waited in line for an open stall, her arms creeping around herself in a self-embrace. Two women in skimpy dresses and stiletto heels were putting on lipstick in front of the mirror.

'I had such a scare last week,' one of them said, her eyes on her own reflection, and Zoe found herself listening, curious despite her own sense of lethargy.

'Oh?' The other woman asked in a rather bored drawl.

'Yes.' She smacked her lips together and slipped her lipstick into her bag. 'My period was three days late, but thank God I wasn't…'

'Pregnant?' The friend filled in as she put her own lipstick away. 'What a nightmare.'

Zoe watched them both sashay out in their spiky heels, and she didn't move until the woman behind her in the queue tapped her on the shoulder. 'Are you in line or what?'

'Oh, sorry,' Zoe mumbled. 'No, I'm not.' She half stumbled out of the bathroom, her mind buzzing.

Such a scare…three days late…thank God I wasn't…
Pregnant.

Pregnant. Pregnant. Pregnant.

The word beat a restless tattoo in her brain. Even in her numb state she could do the math. Her period had been due—what? More than three days ago. Almost five. And she was annoyingly regular, as predictable as clockwork, but—

Max had used a condom. It had just been the one time.

She felt like a teenager, stupid and careless, demanding that this couldn't happen to her, it didn't work that way.

She couldn't be pregnant.

She wasn't, she assured herself. She was stressed, she was unhappy; those things made a difference.

Still, she could hardly stay at the club without the question answered, and without even making her excuses to Karen or any of her friends, she left the pulsing music and flashing strobe lights for the rain-slicked street. She hailed a cab and headed uptown, stopping only at a twenty-four-hour chemist's to pick up the necessary item.

A pregnancy test.

Twenty minutes later, back in the apartment, she stared at two pink lines, and then the leaflet explaining the results. She stared at the lines one more time, and then read the leaflet again. There was no escaping it, no denying it.

She was pregnant. With Max Monroe's baby.

Just the thought of Max made her stomach clench. He'd sent her packing after one night; what on earth would he do when—if—he discovered he was the father of her child?

Yet even as this question formed in Zoe's mind, she realised there was no *if* about it. The life inside of her was tiny, fledgling, but it was there. It was part of her, part of Max, and with a sense of something—her whole self—settling into place, she knew *this* was where she belonged.

And Max needed to know.

It took Zoe three days to work up the courage to face Max. First she had to find him. She couldn't have found her way back to his apartment building if she tried, and she wasn't even sure she wanted to confront Max in the place that was his own domain, where they'd made love. If what they'd done had anything to do with love, which she now knew it hadn't.

Still, it had resulted in a child, a life, and for that alone Zoe knew she had to tell Max. A quick Internet search gave her the address of Monroe Consulting, an office building near Wall Street, right on the water, and Zoe made her way there.

She felt a sickening sense of déjà vu as she crossed the threshold. A row of security desks faced her, guarding the entrance to the elevators which led to the exclusive offices upstairs.

A bored security snapped his gum as he looked up. 'Who are you here to see?'

'Max Monroe.'

The guard nodded and reached for the phone. Zoe watched, her heart thudding as it had before, hardly able to believe that she was in the same awkward, uncomfortable, excruciating position she'd been only three days ago. Once again she was about to confront a hostile man and give him the unwelcome news that he was a father.

And this time it mattered even more.

'Name?' the guard asked, cradling the receiver to his ear, and Zoe swallowed nervously.

'Zoe.' He waited, and she added rather grimly, 'Just Zoe. He'll know who I am.'

The guard shrugged and spoke into the receiver; Zoe couldn't hear what he said. After only a few seconds he replaced the telephone in its cradle. The look of boredom had been replaced by one of prurient interest. Zoe flushed. 'He says he's not expecting you, miss.'

'I didn't ring beforehand,' Zoe confirmed with what she hoped passed as a gracious smile. 'I hope Mr Monroe isn't averse to surprises.'

The guard shrugged. 'He sounds like he might be. He doesn't want to see you anyway.' He paused before he turned back to the newspaper he'd been reading. 'Sorry.'

Zoe stared at the man in disbelief, her flush intensifying, spreading through her entire body in hot, prickly colour. Max Monroe wasn't going to even let her come to his office. He wasn't going to see her at all.

She drew in a shaky breath even as her vision swam and nausea rose in her throat. 'I see,' she managed. 'Thank you.'

On legs that very nearly tottered she made her way out

of the building. She stood in the middle of the concrete concourse in front of the building, the breeze from the Hudson River blowing her hair into tangles around her face. She took two, then three, deep lungfuls of air, trying to steady her nerves, her shaking body. Even now, after one spectacular dismissal, she could hardly believe she'd been given a second. Max Monroe wasn't going to give her the opportunity to tell him about his child.

And she, Zoe determined, was not going to give him the opportunity to escape.

Max sat back in his chair, discomfort prickling along his body, through his thoughts. Why had Zoe—*just* Zoe— come to see him? He'd made it abundantly clear that he had no intention of pursuing a relationship or even setting eyes on her again. He *couldn't*. Yet she'd tracked him down to his office and attempted to gain access—why?

Max had done his best to forget her and the night they'd had together. It took a surprising amount of concentration *not* to think about someone—the scent of her hair, the silken feel of her skin, that unexpected, throaty gurgle of laughter.

And more than that…the way she'd touched him, with such gentle hands, as if she *felt* something. Loved him, even. He still could feel the touch of her lips on his skin, his scar, and the answering agony of need inside of him.

No. He needed to forget, not to remember. There was no future, no hope. Besides, he told himself, rising from his chair in one abrupt yet fluid movement, she wasn't worth his time. She was shallow. Insipid. A vapid, vacuous social butterfly. The only reason she'd been so angry the morning after their night together was because her pride had been hurt. Nothing more.

She probably preferred to be the one to say goodbye.

He had to believe that.

Slowly Max walked to the floor-to-ceiling window to behold a view that was fading all too rapidly. He could see the sun, a golden ball of fire in the sky, glinting off the buildings below, setting the whole world alight.

Only that morning he'd had his regular appointment at the ophthalmologist, to monitor the rate of retinal degeneration.

'You seem to be holding steady,' the doctor had said, as if this were encouragement. Max just shrugged. 'You'll have moments of good, even perfect, vision,' Dr Ayers continued, 'followed by increasing blind spots, floaters and periods of darkness. As I said before, it's not a seamless process.'

'No.' He had experienced those alarming and exhilarating moments where it seemed as if his vision had cleared—as if he could *see*—only to have it all fade to blurry grey again. It felt like a taunt.

Just as knowing Zoe was looking for him felt like a taunt. He wanted to see her again, feel her again, and he couldn't.

He couldn't bear the pain when he failed her, the rejection when *she* was the one to walk away.

The sun had sunk below the horizon of buildings, the Hudson River turning to molten gold with its setting rays, and still Zoe sat on the bench facing the entrance to Max Monroe's building.

She was stiff, chilly and ravenously hungry—not to mention in desperate need of the loo—but she hadn't moved in nearly three hours.

From the moment she'd realised she was carrying this precious little life, she had been certain of one thing: Max would know he was the father. He would be involved.

What shape that might take, how it could possibly happen, Zoe didn't dare to think about. Still, she burned with determination that her baby would not grow up without the knowledge of who her real father was. Like she had.

She—or he—would know. Zoe would make sure of it.

The trouble was, she wasn't sure Max wanted to know. In fact, she was quite sure he didn't.

Just as she was thinking this she saw the man himself. She felt it, a prickle of goose bumps up her arms and along the back of her neck—awareness, alarm, attraction. She watched as he exited the building; he looked stunning and yet grave in his dark suit, a trench coat over one arm. He walked slowly, his steps careful and deliberate in a way that made Zoe's heart ache. He looked, she thought, like a man weighed down by experience, by life itself. What had happened to make Max so burdened?

When he was halfway across the concourse, Zoe stood. He stopped, and they both stood there, staring at each other even as people hurried and scurried around them, silent and waiting.

Max stilled by instinct. The concourse in front of his building was filled with people rushing here and there, hurrying to home or to a restaurant, to a waiting lover or child. Everyone had somebody.

And apparently so did he, at least for this moment, for even though he couldn't see her, he could sense her. Zoe was here, waiting for him. He stilled, and it came to him, the faint scent of rose water. Or was he imagining it? Surely he was, for there was no way he could smell so faint a scent with dozens of people between them.

Where was she?

He walked forward slowly, avoiding the blurred

shapes of people rushing past, letting instinct—and need—guide him.

And then he felt her in front of him, saw for a moment the soft fall of golden hair, the glint of a green eye, the lovely, lovely sound of her voice.

'Max.'

'You're stubborn, aren't you?' He meant to sound cutting but he couldn't quite keep the hint of a smile from his voice.

'I prefer the word *determined*.'

'As you like.' He took a breath, forcing back the words he felt almost desperate to say. *You came back. You smell like spring. Touch me.* 'We have nothing to say to each other, Zoe.' He began to move past her; he could see the dark shape of the waiting limo, his driver at the ready.

'Actually, we do.' She moved quickly—too quickly—in front of him, and he nearly stumbled. Irritation bit at him, making him sound colder than ever.

'Then perhaps I should amend that—*I* have nothing to say to *you*.'

She gave a harsh bark of laughter, a sound like nothing he'd heard before. It was full of bitterness and cynicism, and the realization stabbed him with sorrow. 'Perhaps you will, when you hear what I have to say—'

'I don't—'

'I'm pregnant.'

The two words caused Max to go completely still. They reverberated through his body, his empty soul.

Pregnant. A child. *His* child.

Or not.

His voice was cold and dismissive as he moved past her. 'As I said before, I have nothing to say to you.'

* * *

Zoe watched Max walk away from her in shocked disbelief. Then the fury came, rushing through her in a scalding river, disbelief giving way to determination.

'You're just going to walk away? You're not even going to discuss it?'

He swivelled slowly, stiffly, to address her. 'If you could do simple maths, Zoe, you'd realise not enough time has passed for your pregnancy claim to be credible.' He inclined his head in what she supposed was a gesture of dismissal and started to walk away again.

'I never was very good at maths,' she called to his broad, indifferent back, 'but it's been a few weeks. These days you can take a pregnancy test after just ten days. Plenty of time, Max.'

He stilled again, his back to her. At least thirty seconds ticked by in taut silence. 'Get in the car.'

Zoe saw the limo waiting at the curb, and without a word to Max she stalked to it and threw herself inside.

Max followed, moving with a careful precision that Zoe decided meant he was either very angry or in great pain. Perhaps both.

When the driver had closed the door and began moving through the city's traffic, he spoke.

'You wouldn't have any symptoms yet, and I wore a condom. What on earth made you think to take a pregnancy test?' He turned to her, his grey eyes gleaming in the dim interior of the limo. 'You did take one, I presume?'

'Yes. I overheard some women talking, and I realised I was late, so I—I put two and two together—'

'And came up with an unsavoury three.'

Zoe pressed her hand to her middle. So. The idea of a pregnancy—a child—was *unsavoury* to him. An inconvenience, an irritation. Bitterness spiked her words. 'You've made your feelings clear.'

'Am I supposed to *want* this baby?' he asked in disbelief, and she shook her head.

'No, I suppose that would be too much to ask.' She stared blindly out the window, wondering just why she had come. When she'd learned she was pregnant, it had seemed essential that she tell Max. She wanted her baby to have a father, yet she should have realised Max was hardly going to jump into the role of daddy with eager ease. They barely knew each other.

And the last thing she wanted was for her baby to have a father who rejected her…like she had been rejected.

'What do you want to do?' Max asked eventually, his voice terribly neutral. 'Somehow I don't think you need money, but if that's what you're after—'

Zoe twisted in her seat to glare at him. 'I'm not *after* anything,' she ground out. 'Silly me, I thought it might *concern* you, the fact you've fathered a child.'

Max turned to the window so she couldn't see his expression. 'Are you telling me you intend to keep it?'

Zoe recoiled. 'Would you prefer I didn't?'

He shrugged, not speaking, and revulsion crawled through her. When he finally spoke, it was no more than a whisper, and she couldn't be sure she'd heard him at all. 'No.'

'No?'

'I'm not asking you to get an abortion if you don't wish to have one,' Max said flatly, his face still turned to the window. 'I'm not quite that selfish.'

The limo pulled to the curb in front of Max's building and he got out of the car, leaving Zoe no choice but to follow, tripping once more over the uneven cobbles.

They didn't speak in the foyer, or in the closed space of

the lift as it soared thirty-two floors up into the sky. Zoe waited tensely as Max stalked across his living room—shoving aside a chair in an almost vicious movement—before he poured himself a rather large Scotch and downed it in one gulp.

'I'd offer you a drink but I suppose that's not the thing when you're expecting,' he said, his back to her, his voice dark with a savage humour.

'No, it's all wretched herbal teas,' Zoe replied lightly. 'I'd kill for a cup of coffee.'

'Surely a little caffeine can't be that bad for you, this early on?'

Zoe shrugged. She'd read a brochure that linked excessive caffeine to the threat of a miscarriage, and while the research showed that a cup a day was fine, she realised she didn't want to take unnecessary risks, or even any risks at all.

She wanted this baby. A lot. More than anything she'd ever wanted before. Perhaps even more than she wanted to be a Balfour. The realisation surprised her, and even scared her a little bit.

'So.' Max put his glass down carefully on the table and turned slowly to face her. 'I appreciate you telling me the news, but what exactly are you hoping to achieve here?'

Zoe swallowed. It was, she knew, a good question. What *was* she doing here? What did she want—realistically, possibly—from Max? 'I want you to be involved in our child's life.' The words came out in a nervous rush, and Max arched one eyebrow.

'Involved?' he repeated, and there was no disguising his incredulity. 'What are you talking about?'

His blatant disbelief stung her, reminded her of her own biological father's utter refusal to acknowledge her in any way. 'I'm talking about responsibility, Max—'

'The responsible thing would have been not to get you pregnant in the first place,' Max replied shortly. 'Barring that, it would be to give you the money—'

'No.' Zoe took a step closer to him, her hand pressed against her tummy. 'Are you really that cold-hearted, that you'd wish your own child out of existence?'

Max's face and voice were both expressionless. 'I can't really be sure it's mine, can I?'

'We can have a paternity test as soon as you like,' Zoe said evenly. 'I have nothing to hide.'

'Don't you?' Max remained motionless, but Zoe could still feel his heat, his anger. He stood still, seemingly relaxed, yet to Zoe he felt like a panther ready to pounce. On her. 'Just Zoe?' he jeered softly. 'Who are you, really?'

Zoe met his taunting gaze, her voice steady. 'The woman who is going to have your child.'

Max let out a sharp bark of disbelieving laughter. 'You really are a piece of work.'

'What—'

'Have you even considered what having this baby means, Zoe? What it will do to that lovely little body of yours, to your lifestyle? No more parties, no more late nights. No more spending the night with your latest lover—'

'That's not fair.' Zoe felt the sting of tears under her lids and furiously blinked them away. 'You don't know me—'

'Exactly. I don't know you.' The words seemed to hang in the air, flat and final. 'Do you even know what it means to have a child?' Max demanded after a moment, his voice harsh. 'Or are you just seeing this baby—this life—as another fashion accessory, something different because you're bored?'

Each word, Zoe thought numbly, was a judgement, a condemnation. Of course, there was very little reason for

Max Monroe to think more of her; she hadn't given him any reason to. She hadn't given *anyone* any reason to. And standing there, her face drained of colour, her mouth dry, she wondered at the truth of his words.

Was it selfish—stupid, even—to have a baby because you wanted a family of your own? Because at last you'd have someone to belong to?

Perhaps it was.

Yet even as these thoughts—fears—slipped slyly through her mind, Zoe knew she wanted this baby for more reasons than her own selfish desires. She wanted this baby because it was a child, *her* child, part of her own body, and he or she deserved to live.

'If I wanted a fashion accessory,' she finally said, her voice thankfully dry, 'I'd buy a bracelet.'

Max inclined his head in acknowledgement, and Zoe thought she almost—almost—saw the glimmer of a smile in the curve of his mouth, the flicker in his eyes. Then he shrugged. 'Naturally I'll offer financial support, if that's what you need.'

'Write a cheque and be done with it?'

Max narrowed his eyes. 'What are you angling for, Zoe? Because you can't possibly expect—' He stopped, swallowing, and turned away.

'Expect you to be involved in your child's life? Funny, how men seem to think that idea is so absurd. So impossible.'

Max swung around sharply. 'Are you telling me you've been in this situation before?'

Zoe hesitated. 'In a manner of speaking. But no, I've never been pregnant before.' She took a breath; it hitched slightly. 'I'm not asking you to marry me, Max, or even attempt some kind of godforsaken relationship.' She said the word with a little sneer, even though she didn't feel like sneering. She didn't want a relationship with Max; she was realistic enough to realise how ill-fated that would be. Yet it still hurt that he hadn't even considered it for a moment. He'd dismissed her the morning after they'd made love, and he was dismissing her and her child now.

Hadn't she had enough of rejection? When was she going to wise up and stop insisting on these confrontations? A wave of dizziness passed over and she swayed on her feet, a tiny moan escaping her. Max inhaled sharply.

'Are you all right?'

'I'm just a little dizzy. I haven't eaten in awhile.' She sat down in the nearest chair with an inelegant thud, closing her eyes against the dizziness, the accompanying nausea and, worst of all, the reality of Max's rejection.

Her eyes still closed, she heard him mutter a curse under his breath and he moved from the bar to the kitchen. She heard the sound of cupboards and drawers being opened and shut, and then she opened her eyes to see him at the kitchen counter, its gleaming, pristine surface marred only by the presence of a knife and a jar of peanut butter.

She watched him stand there for a moment, looking lost and a little helpless, and she wondered if he'd actually ever been in his own kitchen.

'I have my meals delivered,' he explained tersely, even though Zoe hadn't said anything. Clearly he must have guessed what she'd been thinking. 'I'm afraid peanut butter and bread is all I have.'

'That's fine.'

He reached for the jar of peanut butter, unscrewing the cap and setting it aside; in the process his elbow knocked the knife from the counter. He cursed again, under his breath. Zoe watched, strangely transfixed, as Max bent, his long, lean fingers slowly sweeping the black marble tiles for the knife. His fingers closed around it after only a few seconds, yet Zoe was left with the odd feeling that he hadn't known where the utensil was.

She opened her mouth to say something—*what?*—but Max's cold, closed expression kept her from uttering a word.

'Thank you,' she finally murmured, for he'd spread peanut butter on two slices of bread and silently handed her a sandwich. She took it, her appetite absolutely vanished, her mind seething with questions. Somehow she felt making a simple sandwich had cost Max something— and she didn't even know what it was.

Was he still injured from his accident? She wanted to ask, but she was uncertain of Max's response. She couldn't bear another rebuff, and actually she wasn't sure she wanted the truth.

Suddenly, she was afraid. Afraid of all the things she didn't know, the future looming dark and so terribly uncertain in front of them both.

'If you're envisioning some kind of happy-families scenario,' Max said after a long, tense moment of silence, 'I'm afraid that it is quite impossible.' He'd moved to the window and propped one shoulder against the wall of glass, seeming utterly indifferent to the spectacular view.

Zoe stared down at her sandwich, unable to manage even a mouthful. 'Impossible?' she repeated slowly, and let it linger in the air, a question.

'Impossible,' Max confirmed. Then, to her surprise, the words seeming reluctant and yet no less heartfelt, he added, 'I'm sorry.'

'You speak as though you have no choice.'

'I don't.' The two words were laced with a surprising and deep regret.

Zoe looked up, eyes flashing, anger—and hurt—

coursing through her. 'What are you saying, Max? You don't want to be involved in this child's life at all?'

His mouth tightened, a muscle flickering in his jaw. 'It's impossible.'

'Only if you choose for it to be so.'

'What are you actually imagining, Zoe?' he demanded harshly, his voice a raw, ragged whisper. 'We barely know each other. I don't even know your last name. Are you actually expecting us to be a *family*?'

That one word—*family*—caused tears to gather under her lids, crowd her throat. She swallowed, blinked, forced it all back. 'I don't know what to expect, Max. All I know is—' She swallowed again, her throat so very tight, and continued. 'I won't let this baby grow up without knowing who her father is.'

He looked at her sharply, as if he wanted to ask a question, and Zoe didn't want to have to explain. She continued in a quieter, more subdued voice. 'And it's Balfour.'

'What?'

'My last name. It's Balfour.'

He shrugged, obviously indifferent and Zoe felt a ridiculous urge to laugh. The name clearly meant nothing to him. That all-important social symbol—a sign of wealth, luxury, prestige and, finally, scandal—was simply a name to Max Monroe. She didn't know whether to be relieved or disappointed; she felt nothing at all.

'At the very least,' she continued, 'you could visit—'

'What? Fly over to England every couple of weeks?'

She blinked, suddenly realising how very little she'd thought any of this out. All she'd thought about since learning she was pregnant—all she'd wanted—was her baby to know her father. To feel as if she belonged, as if she was loved.

Yet you couldn't force either of those. Maybe, Zoe thought hollowly, it would be better for this child not to know her father…if her father didn't want to know her. Yet even as she considered this, she knew it wasn't true. Not knowing, for her, had been as bad as knowing.

Carefully she placed the uneaten sandwich on the table next to her. She rose slowly, dizziness still lapping at the edges of her mind, her self-control a slippery thing. 'I haven't thought any of this through,' she said with as much dignity as she could gather. 'I don't have all the answers, Max, and I won't pretend that I do. I just…' She drew a breath into her lungs, sharp and painful. 'I just wanted this child to know where he or she came from. Because—' She stopped, then forced herself to go on. 'Because I didn't.' Max's mouth opened soundlessly, his eyes widening in surprise, and Zoe hurried on. 'Anyway. It doesn't really matter, does it? Because you can't force the kind of thing I want. You can't force love—not even a father's love for a child. I should know.'

Max closed his eyes briefly; he looked as if he was in pain. 'Zoe—'

'So,' she finished, her voice sounding high and strained, 'that's it. I just wanted you to know.'

He took a deep, shuddering breath and opened his eyes. His face was utterly expressionless, devoid of emotion, and Zoe knew then, with a chill, that he had decided. He'd made up his mind not to be involved. He didn't move, didn't change at all, as he said tonelessly, 'Now I know.'

And he still didn't move as Zoe, on leaden legs, walked slowly to the elevator. She pushed the button, waiting, half expecting or at least hoping for Max to say something. Do something.

He didn't.

It seemed to take ages for the elevator to arrive, yet even so all too soon the doors whooshed open, leaving Zoe with no choice but to step inside. And then, just as once before, they closed, and Max had never said a word.

Max heard the elevator doors close, heard the swoosh as it started downwards. He heard the silence all around him, angry and mocking, and he wished he could close his ears—and heart—against it. He heard Zoe's accusations and, worse, her pleas.

*You can't force love—*not even *a father's love for a child—I should know.*

He didn't know her history, although he supposed he could guess a little bit of it now, and the thought of how he was letting her down—letting their child down—cut through him cleanly. He'd never wanted to let anyone down again. To fail another person was, he knew, the same as failing himself.

Yet better to let her down now—a little—than far more, far worse, later.

You speak as though you have no choice.

Zoe had no idea how true those words were. She'd meant them as an accusation, yet Max felt them as a sentence. A life sentence, impossible to escape. Would Zoe be so eager for him to be involved in their child's life when she learned he was nearly blind, on his way to becoming a virtual invalid? He could imagine her distaste, her horror, at his condition all too well.

And even if she pretended it didn't matter, Max knew it did…to him. To a child. How could he be a father when he couldn't see his child's face? He couldn't play catch with a son; he couldn't whirl a daughter around and around without stumbling, falling, putting her into danger.

He was useless. And worse, far worse, he was afraid.

He choked back another curse, pressing his fists to his eyes, closing them against the bright, blurred shapes. The darkness was complete and almost soothing…for a moment. Then the panic, all too familiar, rose within him, a cry, a silent scream of anguish he'd never voice.

He stalked to the bar, bumping hard into a chair which he shoved out of his way, and reached for the whisky bottle. Here, at least, oblivion—temporary, sweet—could be found.

It was past midnight when he finally stumbled to bed, shedding his clothes with haphazard indifference. Sleep claimed him all too quickly, and with it came the dread and the dreams—the suffocating darkness, the taunts and jeers and, worst of all, the supplications.

Max…do something…help me, please.…

He'd done nothing. He'd sat and waited, unable even to help himself. In his sleep a groan of abject misery escaped him, and he thrashed against the slippery sheets as the memories took hold of him, held him in their vicious grasp.

No…no…please…don't hurt her.…

Help me, Max.…

He hadn't. He hadn't been able to.

As dawn broke, he finally fell into a deeper, dreamless sleep, his muscles still knotted with tension, his eyes clenched closed and his sheets wet with the tears he would never shed while awake.

CHAPTER FIVE

THE next few days passed in a lethargic blur. Zoe didn't go out; she spent most of her days lying in bed, drained and empty. Finally she dragged herself from the apartment, determined to do something. To act.

Yet how? What? She found herself wandering the streets, gazing listlessly at the store fronts and office buildings, watching as people hurried everywhere, busy and productive, part of something. She'd never felt so listless, so separate. Then her gaze fell upon a discreet sign in front of a midrise office building, no different than a thousand others.

Midtown Pregnancy Support Center. Where Women Find the Help They Need.

Without even considering what she was doing, or why, Zoe pushed through the office doors and took the lift to the fourth floor. She entered the support centre, her surprised gaze taking in a few faded, squashy armchairs and a battered desk where a woman was arranging brochures in a basket. She looked up when Zoe entered. 'Can I help?'

'Actually,' Zoe said, and her voice sounded surprisingly strong, 'I was wondering if I could help you.' The woman raised her eyebrows, surprised, and Zoe smiled. 'I'd like to volunteer.'

'Volunteer? Have you been here before?'

'No.' Zoe realised how absurd she must seem, storming in here and asking to be part of it. Yet she wanted to be a part; she wanted to contribute, to act. She needed to *do*, rather than just think and wonder and fear. 'I'm new to the city, but I've got plenty of time on my hands, and I want to do something useful. I know I'm not trained in much of anything,' she continued with determined cheer, 'but I could file and answer phones, surely?'

'Right…' The woman glanced down at the papers on her desk and Zoe felt her tenuous hold on her composure slipping. Please, not another rejection. At this point, she felt as if she might fall apart if someone so much as frowned at her on the street. Then the woman looked up and smiled.

'It's usually so difficult to find volunteers. Everyone is so busy in this city. We'll need to run a few background checks, but I'm sure we'd love your help.' She stuck out her hand. 'I'm Tiffany.'

'Brilliant.' Zoe took her hand and shook it. 'I'm Zoe,' she said, and then added, her voice still strong, 'Zoe Balfour.'

Within a few days Zoe had learned all the menial tasks— from watering the potted plants on the windowsill to making copies of brochures and forms on a rather anti-quated photocopier—that she'd once never have even thought to stoop to. She tried to imagine Holly Mabberly or even Karen seeing her in this setting, and knew they would be incredulous, most likely scornful.

She was, Zoe realised on her third day of volunteering, happy. Or close enough. She knew she'd never be truly happy with the men in her life so indifferent—the men who had actively chosen *not* to be in her life. Yet she was doing something, something good, and that gave her a deep sense of satisfaction she'd never expected to feel.

Yet the nearly eight hours that she put in at the pregnancy centre didn't fill the other long, empty hours of the day and night, hours where she walked through the park, observing the children with their mothers and fathers and nannies, where the sight of a baby dozing contentedly in a pushchair made her insides contract with both hope and fear.

Hours where she lay in bed, exhausted yet sleepless, wistfully imagining a different scenario, a different life, one where her father and the father of her child accepted and embraced her.

Bedtime stories. Fairy tales.

And still there was too much time to think, to wonder, to fear, for she was realising with an increasing sense of panicked urgency that she had no idea what she was doing.

Where would she live? What would she do? How was she going to tell her family, her father? In one grim moment, she pictured the tabloid headlines—*Bastard Gives Birth to Bastard*—and shuddered.

Perhaps she was being foolish, pushing these thoughts away, taking each precious day as it came, enjoying her work at the pregnancy centre, her camaraderie with Tiffany and the other counsellors and volunteers. Yet Zoe knew herself well enough to realise that all the implications and problems of the future would destroy the fragile sense of equanimity she'd finally managed to achieve.

Then the sickness hit. She'd been feeling a little queasy off and on, but nothing like the utter wretchedness that descended on her just a little over a week after she last saw Max. Exhausted and utterly nauseous, she took several days off volunteering and spent them in bed, nibbling on dry crackers and trying to sleep as much as she could.

One dreary, drizzly afternoon the doorbell rang and, thinking it must be the housekeeper, Lila, forgetting her key, she roused herself from her state of lethargy and went to open the front door.

It wasn't Lila. It was Max.

Zoe's mouth dropped open in shock as she stared at him; his hair was damp from rain, and he wore an exquisitely cut grey suit, the steely colour matching his eyes. He looked grim, determined and resolute—and absolutely wonderful.

Zoe's heart bumped against her ribs and she was suddenly, painfully conscious of how she looked. She hadn't showered, her hair was in a scraggly mess and she was wearing the comfort pyjamas that nobody ever saw her in. Max, however, didn't seem to notice, and he made no comment. Still, she folded her arms across her chest in a gesture of self-protection.

'What are you doing here?'

'We need to talk.'

Zoe arched an eyebrow in cool scepticism even as her heart lurched. 'Oh, really?'

'Yes, really,' Max snapped. 'Now are you going to let me inside?'

'Since you asked so graciously,' Zoe muttered, and stepped aside. She watched as Max walked slowly into the foyer, gazing around at the priceless antiques—her father had a passion for ancient art and sculpture—with something close to disdain.

The scornful look on his face made Zoe's own cheeks burn with shame and resentment. Had he learned of her own birth? It would have only taken the most rudimentary Internet search to discover who she was; she'd given him the ammunition when she'd told him her full name. Was that why he looked so contemptuous now, because he knew who she was? He knew she didn't belong here, didn't deserve—

Zoe clamped down on these thoughts and gazed levelly at Max. 'What do you want?'

'Are we going to be so uncivilised as to stand here in the hall?'

'You're hardly one to speak of civility,' Zoe fired back.

Max inclined his head in acknowledgement. 'I'm sorry.'

Surprised, it took Zoe a moment to find her tongue. 'You said that before.'

'You shocked me. I spoke out of turn.' The words were spoken flatly, without emotion, yet their meaning made Zoe's heart turn. Was he having second thoughts? Good ones?

'Follow me.' She turned and led the way into the living room, with its thick Aubusson carpet and its sweeping view of Central Park. After the slightest hesitation, Max followed.

'I'm sorry I look such a fright,' Zoe said in what she hoped was a flippant tone. 'If I'd known you were coming, I would have taken a bit more care.'

Max just shrugged. 'It's not important.' He cleared his throat. 'Have you been feeling well?'

Zoe let out a disbelieving laugh. 'You see me like this and you can ask that? No, I've been feeling wretched.'

'I'm sorry,' Max said after a moment.

'It's meant to pass in a few weeks,' Zoe replied. 'I think.' They both lapsed into a tense, uneasy silence. Max stood in the centre of the room, unmoving, his face so terribly expressionless. Zoe had no idea what he was thinking, wanting. Wearily she pushed a tangled mass of hair behind one ear and asked, 'Why are you here, Max?'

He turned slowly to face her, his body tense and straight, shoulders thrown back, chin angled haughtily, yet even so Zoe wondered if she saw a shadow of vulnerability in his dark eyes. Or was she just being fanciful, hoping for some more tender emotion that wasn't there?

'I told you, I spoke out of turn the other day,' Max said tightly. 'I…I shouldn't have dismissed you quite so readily.'

Was that actually meant to be an apology? Zoe wondered. 'Thanks for that,' she said, not bothering to hide her sarcasm. 'It didn't take you long to realise you were an utter cad—'

'I was surprised,' Max cut her off, his voice sharpening. 'And I still don't know how—' He stopped, his lips pressed tightly together, and Zoe felt a thrill of trepidation ripple coldly through her.

'How what?' she asked quietly.

'How any of this will work, if you actually intend to have this baby,' Max snapped. 'We're *strangers*, Zoe—'

'Strangers who slept together.' She couldn't quite hide the note of sorrow from her voice. Max simply shrugged and Zoe drew herself up. 'So what exactly are you proposing?' she asked, then winced at her choice of words.

'I'm not *proposing* anything,' Max returned evenly. 'But if you are indeed having my child, then naturally I have a certain responsibility.' He made it sound so cold, so heartless, a matter of duty, not desire, yet Zoe knew she couldn't really expect much more. 'Are you planning on remaining in New York for the duration of your pregnancy?'

'I…I haven't thought…' Zoe pleated the worn fabric of her track bottoms between her fingers. She hadn't thought through anything, yet she knew she couldn't return to England—not yet, not when the tabloid's rabid eye would be trained so viciously on her, especially if anyone learned she was pregnant. 'I think I should stay here,' she said after a moment, and heard the hesitation and uncertainty in her voice.

'Is there a reason why you don't want to return to England?' Max asked, his tone neutral, but nerves and fear made Zoe spiky. 'You mentioned—'

'I just want to stay here,' Zoe cut him off, and Max nodded. He wasn't going to press, Zoe realised with a wave of relief. At least not yet.

'Fine. Have you seen a doctor?' he asked after a moment.

'No, not yet. It's still early days.'

'Yet if you're feeling wretched, surely there is something a doctor could prescribe.'

'I don't know—' Zoe admitted. She watched as Max withdrew a slim mobile phone from his breast pocket and began to punch in numbers. 'What are you—?'

He spoke tersely into the mobile, and Zoe realised he must be talking to some assistant, a staff member ready to scurry and obey his sharply given commands. He snapped the phone shut. 'My assistant is looking into doctors. We'll try to get an appointment for this afternoon.'

Zoe was torn between annoyance, admiration and a strange sort of gratitude. When he put his mind to it, he obviously got things done, but she wasn't sure she wanted to be quite so *managed*. 'I'm fine—'

'You said you were feeling wretched,' Max pointed out, and then had the gall to actually sniff. 'Perhaps you'd like to shower before your appointment?'

Mortified, Zoe flushed to the roots of her unwashed hair. Surely she didn't actually *smell*? 'Fine,' she said stiffly. She rose from her chair; Max hadn't moved from his militarylike stance in the centre of the room. 'Are you just going to wait here?' He shrugged one powerful shoulder and Zoe couldn't help but ask a bit resentfully, 'Don't you have things to do? Money to make?'

Max gave her the faintest flicker of a smile. 'The good thing about making money,' he said, 'is that after awhile it makes more all on its own.' He shoved one hand in his trouser pocket, looking a shade more relaxed. 'I have time.'

She should be glad Max was here, Zoe knew, grateful that he'd changed his mind and wanted to be involved in some way. Yet for some perverse reason she could only feel resentful. He changed his mind, and now she was meant to leap to do his bidding? She felt like a parcel to be cared for, rather than a person.

The shower felt good, stinging and hot, and despite her queasy stomach she felt a bit better, enough to dress with care in a pair of skinny jeans—she could still fit into them, although the zip stuck a bit in the middle—knee-high leather boots and a silky T-shirt the colour of sea foam. She did her make-up, knowing she was being ridiculously vain, wanting to look good for Max. She doubted he would even notice, and yet still she was ludicrously disappointed when she returned to the living room and he didn't even glance at her.

'We have an appointment in an hour,' Max said briskly. 'My car will be here in five minutes.'

'That was quick,' Zoe said a bit sulkily. 'Amazing how you can get things done when you put your mind to it.' She knew she sounded sharp and sarcastic and didn't really care.

Max fixed her with a cool, even stare. 'I understand why you're angry with me, Zoe. I didn't behave as I should have—as I wanted to—the last time we spoke. I'm sorry. But I'm doing my best now to take care of you and our child, and I'd appreciate not having it tossed back at me at every turn.' He spoke levelly, his face expressionless, and Zoe nodded in acceptance.

'I suppose this situation is difficult for us both.'

'Indeed.' He reached out an arm, and belatedly Zoe realised she was meant to take it. She slipped her arm through his awkwardly, conscious of his nearness, the scent of his aftershave, something woodsy and clean, and a deeper, muskier smell underneath that was surely just him.

His arm felt strong under hers, the muscles rippling beneath the smooth fabric of his suit, and for a second Zoe wanted to lean into him, to feel the strength of him as she had before, that night. She wanted to lean on someone— on him—and admit that she was uncertain and afraid, that the future scared her, that she really had no idea what she was doing or who she was. That she was *trying*—and this baby felt right, the first right thing in a long time—but she was still afraid of failing. Of messing up. Of losing— losing even Max himself, which was ridiculous, because she'd never even had him in the first place.

Perhaps Max could guess some of her thoughts already; perhaps he would only feel contempt if she admitted such weaknesses to him. He probably didn't have a moment of weakness, she thought with a touch of resentment. He always seemed so self-assured, so collected, so certain of his place in the world.

The moment when Zoe had kissed his scar—the moonlight rippling over them in a silver curtain of light—slipped into her mind and she found herself thinking that Max hadn't been so sure then. Yet the man who had let her kiss him, hold him…that man had disappeared. Zoe didn't even know if he was real, or if she'd ever see him again.

They might have once been lovers, but they weren't now. Now, Zoe acknowledged starkly, they were bound together by only one thing—the baby nestled in her womb.

Max tried not to lean on Zoe's arm, not to inhale the sweet scent of her hair, her skin. *Roses.* Tried not to show any weakness, or the fact that coming here, to a strange place, to her, had taken every ounce of his strength and self-control. New places challenged him now. Hell, they *scared* him. He could make out vague shapes, doorways and corners, but too much could trip him up. Every step felt as if he were about to fall into a void of unknowing. He didn't want to stumble. He didn't want to fall.

He didn't, he knew, want to make an ass of himself, or have Zoe realise that he was near blind.

Yet she would surely have to know at some point, if she didn't figure it out on her own. He would have to tell her; he could hardly keep such a secret if they were to be involved in any way. Already his mind jumped ahead to the future, wondering just who Zoe Balfour was. If, despite her social connections, her beauty and her charm, she was the kind of woman who could live with a blind man.

Who could love him.

You think this is about love? his mind—and perhaps his heart—slyly mocked. *What do you want from her? What can you really expect from her?*

Nothing was the only answer to both of those questions.

The limo was waiting by the curb; Max could make out its long, dark shape, and he heard the door open and close, his driver calling out.

'Mr Monroe.'

Frank knew about his lost eyesight; Max had been forced to tell him when he'd been unable to perform the smallest, simplest tasks that he'd taken for granted before. Now they never spoke of it, but Frank performed small services that were indispensable—he spoke as he opened the door so Max would know where he was; he made sure the way to the car was clear. Max relied on him utterly, and the knowledge stung. He'd been independent, needing no one for so long, and now he was nearly as helpless as the child he and Zoe would soon have.

What would Zoe think then? And why should he even care? No, he didn't want to be pitied, but he could surely deal with it, or even with her scorn. It didn't have to matter;

he didn't have to *care*. And he could still be involved in his child's life.

It was that realisation that had brought him back to Zoe. After she'd left his apartment, regret and guilt had lashed at him. In his own agony of disappointment, he'd treated her without care or concern, or, if he were honest, even the least amount of sensitivity.

During the long, dark nights, as he staved off sleep and its accompanying dreams, he'd thought of her. He'd imagined he could still smell her on his sheets. He'd pictured their baby, for some reason a girl; she would have blonde curls and Zoe's jade-green eyes. He wouldn't be able to see this baby with his eyes, but he'd felt, during those long, lonely nights, that he could already see her with his heart.

Then he chastised and mocked himself for such ridiculous, fanciful, sentimental dreams. He barely knew Zoe—Zoe Balfour, apparently—and what he knew of her suggested that she would be horrified by his liability, his weakness. No matter what he secretly might long for in those dark, weak moments, he knew he couldn't be involved with Zoe Balfour.

Even so his code of honour, latent all these weeks of blasted self-pity, would not allow his own child to enter this world fatherless. He'd let someone down before, terribly, totally, out of weakness and fear, and he wouldn't do it again. Ever. Not Zoe, not his child. No matter what cost.

And so he'd searched Zoe out, and he would care for both her and her child—*his* child—even if it meant enduring her pity or scorn.

Still, he had no idea what it would look like, how it would feel, what it could mean.

Or when—how—he could tell Zoe about his blindness.

* * *

Zoe leant her head back against the plush leather seat and closed her eyes as the limo sped down Park Avenue, the speed making her already queasy tummy do another alarming lurch.

Max had been staring ahead, seemingly oblivious of her since they'd entered the limo, and Zoe gathered he didn't want to talk. Well, neither did she; this situation was awkward enough without enduring pointless, stilted conversations.

A knot of misery lodged in her gut, found its way up her throat. She'd clung to the belief—the hope—that her child would know its father, and now Max was choosing to make that a reality, so why couldn't she be happier?

Why did everything still feel so unsettled, so *wrong*?

Zoe glanced at the forbidding profile of the man seated next to her and knew why she felt as unhappy as she did. Max might be willing to care for her and her child, but he obviously didn't like it. Right now he looked as if he'd rather be anywhere—with anyone else—in the world.

Sighing, Zoe turned away and closed her eyes once more.

The doctor Max had found came highly recommended—or so he told her—yet Zoe could barely summon the energy to care or even respond as she sat in the luxurious waiting room, flipping through celebrity gossip magazines with a listless air.

Max sat next to her, his body rigid, his expression forbidding. Zoe fished out a packet of crackers from her handbag and nibbled one miserably.

When they were finally called into the examining room, she perched on the edge of the table with its crackly paper, suddenly nervous and unsure. The thought of being physically examined with Max standing in the corner of the room like a dark shadow made her feel even more nauseous than usual.

Perhaps he sensed this, for he suddenly asked, his

voice as terse as ever, 'Would you prefer me to be in the waiting room?'

'I...' Zoe swallowed, moistening her lips. 'No. It's all right. You can stay.' Stupidly, perhaps, she meant it.

A few minutes later Dr Hargreaves, a trim, grey-haired woman in her early fifties, entered the room. 'Mrs Monroe?'

'No—' The word came from Zoe involuntarily, horror and humiliation making her face burn. She glanced at Max, who didn't react. 'That is...my name is Zoe. Zoe Balfour. I'm— We're...not—'

'Of course,' Dr Hargreaves said smoothly. 'I apologise for my assumption. The assistant who took Mr Monroe's call must have made a mistake.' She smiled briskly and took Zoe's chart from the folder by the door. 'Now, let's see...your last period was about eight weeks ago?'

'I...I think so.' Zoe couldn't look at Max, which was just as well because he was standing utterly still and silent, the look on his face still so forbidding.

'And you've done a home test?'

'Yes.'

'And you're feeling quite nauseous?' The doctor continued with sympathy. 'It tends to hit right around this time.'

'Right.'

She flicked a glance towards Max. 'I can prescribe something to help the nausea if it's really bad, but the best thing is to eat protein, especially early in the morning, and snack frequently. It does usually pass within a few weeks.'

'Good to know.' Zoe smiled weakly, so achingly conscious of Max standing there, arms crossed, face so damned inscrutable.

'Now we can't hear the heartbeat yet with the Doppler as it's so early, but I can do a quick scan to reassure you?' Dr Hargreaves smiled, and Zoe thought she saw a compassion in the woman's kind eyes; the tension in the room, between her and Max, was surely palpable enough for the doctor to feel it. 'We might be able to see the heartbeat, at any rate.'

'That would be wonderful.'

Zoe stretched out on the table, and Dr Hargreaves squeezed some cold, clear gel on her tummy. She switched on the ultrasound equipment and began to sweep the wand over her middle.

It seemed to take an age, and Zoe felt her hands turn clammy and her heart thud with fear, but then Dr Hargreaves smiled. 'Ah. There it is. Do you see?'

And amazingly, she did see: a tiny, perfect little bean of a baby, with a heart beating like a butterfly's wing. There really was a baby in there. Zoe laughed aloud, a sound of wonder and disbelief, but when she looked at Max she saw he wasn't even glancing at the ultrasound screen.

Dr Hargreaves switched on the sound, and the room was suddenly filled with the quick, thready sound of their baby's heart. 'Sounds a bit like a horse galloping,' she said with a smile, and Zoe nodded. It was a wonderful sound, the sound of life, and when she looked at Max again she saw with surprise that his face, so expressionless before, was now suffused with emotion. It took her a moment to realise what was reflected in his eyes, in the incredulous curve of his mouth. It was joy. He was smiling, and with a ripple of shock Zoe realised his eyes were damp. He blinked hard.

Without even seeming to realise what he was doing, Max reached out his hand, his fingers fumbling for hers, and then lacing with them tightly. She leant her head back against the hard little pillow and closed her eyes, a sudden sense of overwhelming relief making her faint and dizzy with the sheer hope and joy of it. *It's going to be all right,* she thought, her hand still held tightly in Max's. *I don't know how, or even what, but it's going to be all right.*

Max kept holding her hand even as Dr Hargreaves switched off the ultrasound machine and handed Zoe a paper towel to wipe the gel off her stomach.

'I never get tired of the sound,' she said cheerfully. 'So everything looks as if it progressing normally—you should schedule another visit in about four weeks, although of course if you have concerns I can see you earlier. And if you like I'll prescribe something to help with the nausea.'

Zoe nodded, and glanced again at Max, wondering how he was taking all this. Despite the wonder of the moment before—despite the fact that he was still holding her hand—she felt afraid and uncertain. Four weeks suddenly sounded like a long time. So did nine months.

Max must have been thinking along the same lines, for he slipped his hand from hers and he retreated to the corner, unmoving, the smile wiped from his face completely so that once again Zoe had no idea what he was thinking or feeling.

They didn't speak as they left the doctor's office. Max's limo was waiting by the curb, and they both climbed silently inside, speeding down Park Avenue in a tense, uneasy silence.

As the traffic lights passed in a blur of green, block after block of brownstones, Zoe finally worked up the nerve to speak. 'So.' She cleared her throat. 'Thank you for arranging the doctor's visit. It was wonderful to see the heartbeat.'

'And hear it,' Max agreed quietly. He paused, flexing his fingers as if he was remembering how they felt holding hers. Or was she just imagining that? Hoping it? 'I think we should celebrate.'

'What?' Startled, incredulous, Zoe could only stare at him.

Max smiled, his mouth flicking upwards, a teasing glint in his eye that Zoe had never seen before.

'It's not every day you hear your baby's heartbeat. And no matter what has happened before—' He paused, sounding stilted. 'No matter what is—or isn't—between us, we can celebrate that. A life. A new life.' He sounded wistful, even aching, and yet determined.

Zoe smiled. 'That's true. What shall we do?'

'Dinner,' Max said firmly, 'at Le Cirque.'

'I'm not dressed—'

'We can stop by your apartment,' Max told her. 'I'm sure you have something fabulous.'

An hour later, feeling slightly unreal—and far too hopeful—Zoe slipped back into Max's limo. She wore an evening gown in silver satin, one of her favourite dresses. It was simple, deceptively so, falling from two skinny straps to skim her growing curves and swirl around her ankles. She left her hair full and loose over her shoulders, and when Max first saw her he smiled faintly and said, 'Silver.'

Zoe had smoothed the gown over her hips and smiled self-consciously. 'Yes, it's a bit bright, I suppose—'

'I like it,' Max said firmly, and led her to the waiting limo.

It was early for dinner, and the restaurant was nearly deserted. Still, Max insisted on a private table in the corner, and the intimacy felt new, strange. She picked up the heavy gilt menu and stared blindly at the entrées. What was going on here? she wondered. Was this actually a date? She was stunned by Max's seeming about-face, hopeful that it could lead to better things, more things. That they could have some kind of future.

The waiter came, and Max ordered champagne. Zoe opened her mouth to protest but he held up a hand. 'I know you're not supposed to have any alcohol, but you can surely have a sip at least.'

'I suppose.' She clenched her napkin in her lap, feeling nervous and shy. 'I didn't expect you to want to celebrate…this.'

Max's answering smile was wry. 'I didn't expect it either. I know—' He sighed and ran a hand through his hair. 'I know I was a complete idiot before. I'm—I'm trying not to be.' He gave a little laugh. 'That's not much, is it?'

Zoe smiled. Max's confession had the odd effect of lightening everything inside her, dissolving—if only for the moment—her worries and fears. 'It's more than you think.'

'I want to celebrate,' Max told her. His voice was low and strangely fierce. 'I want to remember the good things.'

Zoe tilted her head, unnerved by the fierce resolve in his voice. He sounded almost as if he were speaking about the past rather than the future. The waiter came then with the champagne, and made a show of opening the bottle, the cork popping and bubbles frothing over.

Max lifted his glass, and so did Zoe. 'To the future.'

It was a rather open-ended toast, Zoe thought, but at least Max thought there was a future. For them. 'To the future,' she echoed, and took a tiny sip.

After they'd ordered, a silence seemed to descend on them, heavy and awkward. Zoe was conscious of how little they knew each other. She pleated her napkin in her lap, ridiculously tongue-tied. She could flirt famously, banter with the best, and yet now she found she had nothing to say. Or perhaps she had too much to say, and none of the courage to actually say it.

'So,' Max said after a moment. 'Zoe Balfour.' Zoe tensed, waiting. 'You're from quite a famous family.' Words crowded in her throat so she could only manage a jerky nod. 'I'd never heard of you, of course,' Max continued insouciantly, and Zoe gave a little gurgle of laughter.

'No?'

'But apparently you've got a family manor in England and a million sisters…or so a search on the Internet shows.'

'Really? Did it tell you anything else?' she asked, bracing herself for what else it might reveal.

Max shook his head. 'No, just your family name.' He smiled. 'Sorry, you're not that important.'

'Shame.' She waited, expecting him to ask more. Know more. Yet he didn't say anything, and even as she felt a flicker of relief, she found herself saying, 'Actually, it's not really my family name.'

Max cocked his head, his expression alert and watchful. Waiting. Zoe forced herself to continue, unsure why she'd begun this in the first place, and yet knowing she wanted to say it. She wanted Max to know.

'I'm illegitimate. You probably heard—read about it, if you did some kind of Internet search.'

'There were a few mentions of that,' Max agreed quietly. Zoe tried to smile.

'Just a few? I must really not be important.'

He smiled faintly.

'I just found out a few weeks ago—well, a few months now, I suppose.' She stared down at her lap, a lump of painful emotion lodging in her throat.

'That must have been hard,' Max said quietly. Simple words, yet Zoe knew he meant them. She felt he understood, and his words were a balm.

'It was. It still is. I suppose that's why I was so determined to find you—for this baby to know you. I don't want her—or him—to wonder. I don't want there to be secrets.'

'There won't be.'

Zoe nodded, her throat tight—too tight. She wanted to ask him how. Why. She wanted details, plans, promises. She knew neither of them were ready for any of those. They barely knew each other, and while tonight was wonderful, it was also fragile. It wasn't ready to be tested.

They kept the conversation light and impersonal as they ate their dinner, yet even so Zoe enjoyed the talk of weather, films, the best restaurants and museums in New York. She found herself beginning to banter, even to flirt, and she liked that her old self was still there. She wasn't completely changed.

By the time dessert came round, the restaurant had started to fill up and a jazz quartet was playing near a small dance floor that was, Zoe saw, completely empty. Yet she felt reckless, hopeful, and so she tossed her napkin on the table.

'Let's dance.'

Max froze. 'What?'

She gestured to the dance floor, still buoyant. 'Come on, Max. We're celebrating, remember? Let's dance.'

Max couldn't quite see Zoe's face, but he could feel the energy and enthusiasm rolling off her in intoxicating waves and he was reluctant to quench them. He was also reluctant to make a complete fool of himself. He couldn't dance. His fingers clenched on the napkin in his lap.

'I don't dance.'

He felt rather than saw Zoe's disappointment and uncertainty. 'Come on, Max,' she said lightly, although he heard the yearning underneath. 'I bet you could really cut up the rug if you wanted to.'

The image was ludicrous. He smiled faintly. 'I don't think so.'

'No? You're not a dancer?' She still sounded light but

Max could tell she was hurt. He felt like a cad. Worse, he shared her disappointment because he couldn't remember the last time he'd enjoyed himself so much. Tonight he'd felt free, unburdened. Happy. Hopeful. He wasn't going to give that up so easily, even if it meant he might look like a fool.

'Well, I suppose there's a first for everything.' He tossed his napkin on the table and rose stiffly, the restaurant seeming to stretch endlessly in every direction, full of unknown obstacles, hidden dangers. Smiling, he held out his hand. 'Shall we?'

Zoe rose and slipped her hand into his and Max laced his fingers with hers, remembering how he'd held her hand at the doctor's office, how he'd wanted to. He still wanted to, and he needed her strength. She was his anchor as they wove through the sea of tables to the relatively safe stretch of dance floor.

A lone saxophone wailed soulfully, and Max knew very little dancing would be required. What was dancing but an excuse to hold someone? And he wanted to hold Zoe. He reached for her, glad and grateful that she slid into his embrace naturally and without reserve. For a split second their bodies remained apart, separate and untouching, and then by mutual accord Zoe nestled into him, her body pliant and seeming to fit around his so perfectly. Max rested his head on her hair, one hand on the gentle curve of her hip, the other laced with her own. They barely moved, merely swayed and shuffled. It was enough; it was more than enough.

It was wonderful.

Max didn't know how long they danced; it could have been minutes or even hours. He was conscious of nothing, of no one but Zoe and the feel of her against him. It felt like home and heaven all at once.

At some point he felt instinctively that she was tired, and he remembered with a pang that she was pregnant, that only this morning she'd been nearly too nauseous even to leave the apartment.

He stepped away, steadying her with one hand. 'It's late. I should get you home.'

'I am tired,' Zoe admitted with a little laugh. 'But I feel like dancing forever.'

So do I, Max thought, but somehow he couldn't say the words. Now that they weren't dancing he felt the old fear come back. The restaurant seemed to yawn menacingly around them, and the walk back to their table and then outside to the car felt as arduous and impossible as climbing a mountain. As impossible as having a relationship with a woman as beautiful and desirable as Zoe Balfour. He would have to tell her about his blindness at some point, yet Max knew it wasn't even about saying the words.

It was about building that trust, allowing himself to be honest, to hope, perhaps even to love. Opening himself up to pain, and opening Zoe to pain.

As terrifying as the prospect of her not giving him a chance was the possibility that she would.

What if he failed her?

He would, Max thought bleakly, rather not try—or love—at all.

Despite her fatigue and nausea, Zoe practically floated out to the limo. Her whole body tingled from their dancing, where Max had touched her. He'd been a different man tonight, she thought almost dreamily. He'd been the man she'd first seen, the man she'd hoped she'd seen, and even *better* than that.

Her body hummed. Her mind flew to distant possibilities, dreams she'd hardly acknowledged until now. Dreams of a family, of her and Max…

'I want you to come with me,' Max said. They were riding in the limo, cars streaming past, the night still dark around them. Zoe turned to him, startled.

'Where?' she asked, knowing at this moment she'd go with him anywhere.

He smiled faintly, although Zoe felt something sad emanating from him and it made her a little afraid. She half reached out to him, but then dropped her hand at the last moment. Afraid, even now. Especially now. 'To the Hamptons,' Max said, and Zoe's heart swelled with hope.

'Of course,' she said simply, and they didn't speak again except to say goodbye.

CHAPTER SIX

She should refuse, Zoe thought. That would be the sensible thing to do. She barely knew Max. One dance did not change everything, even if it felt as if it had. He'd been harsh, judgemental, even cruel. Going on their track record, she should not trot after him to the Hamptons as soon as he crooked his finger. The very idea was absurd and unreasonable.

So why, Zoe asked herself, had she agreed so absolutely, felt the certainty of her own decision deep in her bones? Why had she rung the pregnancy centre to say she wouldn't be volunteering for at least a week? Why was she, in fact, packing her bags?

Why was she now staring out the window at the stream of taxis speeding by, counting the minutes until Max came to pick her up? Why was she looking forward to this unexpected and unexplained trip with excitement and, more damning still, *hope*?

What on earth was there to hope for?

He held my hand. He danced with me. She blew out an exasperated breath, feeling as stupid and naive as a little girl who believed in fairy tales. Happy endings. A few little kindnesses did not change the cold, hard fact that they barely knew each other, and Max had not even given a hint as to how he thought he would be involved in their baby's life. In her life.

She had no idea what was going to happen, or even what she wanted to happen.

I could love him.

'No.' She spoke out loud, the treacherous thought slipping from her mind so softly, so dangerously. Love was dangerous. Loving someone like Max—someone she didn't completely understand—was way too much of a risk. She'd been rejected too many times recently; she surely couldn't think of taking the biggest risk of all.

Her whole heart.

No.

Max's limo pulled to the curb, and Zoe's fruitless, fearful questioning ground to a halt as her heart skipped a beat and her hands grew clammy with nerves. She watched as Max exited the limousine, walked with his deliberate, measured strides to the entrance of her building.

The doorman didn't ring up, just as he hadn't the last time Max had visited. Max, Zoe realised, had the kind of imposing presence that quailed even Park Avenue's premier doormen, and kept them from the kinds of security checks he so obviously didn't require.

When the front bell finally buzzed, Zoe knew it was Max himself and she went to open the door with both trepidation and joy—a heady, uncomfortable and even dangerous mix.

Max stood there, dressed with casual elegance in a white button-down shirt and pressed khakis. He stared straight ahead, his expression rather grim.

'Zoe?' he said, and for a tiny second Zoe thought he almost sounded uncertain.

'Yes.'

'Are you ready?' There was a bite of impatience in his

voice now, and to her annoyance Zoe realised she was flushing. Any intimacy they'd shared the night before seemed to have evaporated in the glare of day. Zoe found it hard to believe that he'd held her, that she'd nestled close to his body as if she'd always belonged there.

'Yes. Of course. I'll just get my bag.'

'I'll carry it.' After a second's pause he stepped forward, and it took Zoe a moment to realise he was waiting to tell her where it was. She felt awkward, gauche even, clumsy and uncertain.

'It's right here.' She reached for the handle of a suitcase that was far too large—she'd ended up packing most of her wardrobe, even the outfits that were sadly becoming a little too tight.

'I told you, I'll do it,' Max said, and hefted the heavy case with ease.

Zoe followed him out of the apartment, into the lift and then downstairs and outside into the warm sunshine. Neither of them spoke.

Max's driver took her suitcase and Zoe slid inside the limo, Max following her. His thigh pressed against hers as he sat down, and Zoe tingled from his touch, no matter it was obviously inadvertent, for he muttered some kind of apology and moved closer to the window. What had happened to last night, when he'd gathered her to him, when he'd wanted to touch her?

What had changed?

Zoe couldn't answer for Max, but she knew that, for herself, fear replaced hope. Doubt took over from certainty, and she was left huddling near the window in silent near-misery.

The limo sped away from the curb, and within minutes they were leaving the endless city blocks behind them for the Lincoln Tunnel, and then the golden stretch of highway towards Long Island Sound.

Zoe leant her head back against the seat, nerves making her queasier than usual, her heart still racing and skipping as skittishly as a newborn foal. Max remained brooding and silent, and she couldn't even begin to think what to say. What to feel. The situation was so bizarre, so strange and unexpected, and yet still—even now—so hopeful.

It was there, a precious seed, determined to take root, determined to believe that even if this was the mess Max claimed it was, even if they were two damaged and broken strangers whose only tie was the child she carried, even if she was afraid Max wouldn't—couldn't—love her, *even if*...

There was *some* way forward. Max had said so himself.

Despite the tension in the car, Zoe drifted into a doze without realising, for she found herself blinking sleep from her eyes as the limo slowed to a stop. Outside the sky was hard and blue, glinting brightly off the water.

The limo was parked in front of a sprawling, shingled beach house perched on a bluff overlooking the sound. Zoe glanced around and couldn't see another house or building, just scrub and sand. The limo, she realised, had come down a narrow, sandy track, and this was its end.

'This looks like the last house on all of Long Island,' she joked as she slid from the car and stretched, her muscles aching, her stomach still queasy...although Zoe wondered how much this nausea had to do with pregnancy.

She was nervous, she realised. She was afraid—of what? Not of Max, even though his expression was shuttered, his eyes dark; not of the house, which looked beautiful, jutting out to sea; not even of the future, which loomed in front of her, uncertain, unknowable.

No, she was afraid of herself, afraid of the longing this

man created inside her, a deep well of need she didn't even understand. Why her? Why Max? Why did her body and soul and perhaps even heart long for something from a man who was so obviously inappropriate and unwilling to give it?

Why now?

Her hands went to the small of her back, where a persistent knot of tension had lodged.

'Are you all right?' Max asked, his tone all too polite.

'Just tired.'

'Come inside.'

He turned and walked up the slate path that wound through a landscaped garden of rhododendrons and hydrangeas, his steps measured and precise. Zoe followed, gazing out at the winking sea, a few sailboats bobbing lazily in the distance, the air fresh with the tang of brine, and felt that little seed of hope nestle inside her soul and start to unfurl.

Inside, the house was all light and space, every window providing a breathtaking vantage point to view the sea and sky. The foyer soared upwards, lit by an immense skylight, bathing the room with the warmth and brightness of the sun.

Zoe's footsteps echoed on the polished marble floor, and she felt the emptiness of the rooms around her.

'Are we alone?'

Max had dropped his keys on the hall table and shrugged out of his suit jacket. Zoe watched in helpless fascination at the ripple of muscles under the smooth, expensive fabric of his shirt and felt a tug of desire—and remembered longing—deep in her belly.

'Yes. There's a live-in housekeeper but she's on vacation at the moment.' He paused. 'I thought we might as well manage for ourselves.'

'OK.' Zoe tried to keep her voice light and unconcerned

even though the thought of being alone with Max made her stomach dip yet again. 'I have to warn you, I'm not much of a cook.'

'I wouldn't expect you to be. We can order in.' He turned to her, the glimmer of a smile on his face, flickering in his eyes. 'Any cravings yet?'

'Actually, I could kill for a good tikka masala,' Zoe admitted with a little laugh. 'And I don't even like Indian food all that much.'

'Consider it done.' He turned away from her, and Zoe felt ridiculously bereft, as if he'd somehow withdrawn from her even though he was still in the room, still only a few feet away. Words crowded and clogged in her throat.

Why are you so distant? What changed you from the man you were last night? Which man were you last night? And then, surprising her, *Who am I? I feel like I may have found myself here, and yet I'm not even sure who that is.* Who could she be, in relation to Max, if not Zoe Balfour? The Zoe Balfour the world knew, the Zoe Balfour she knew.

'You should rest,' he told her. 'You can have any bedroom you like upstairs.' Already he was walking away. 'I'll see you at dinnertime.'

Max walked stiffly away, forcing back the stupid feeling of regret at leaving Zoe alone. He'd brought her here because he'd wanted to, because he needed to. He'd told himself they needed to spend time together, if simply to figure out where they were going. What kind of future they could have. Yet now that she was here, observing him, *seeing* him, he realised he couldn't bear the thought of her seeing him unguarded, vulnerable. Knowing the truth.

He had work to occupy him, at least, several conference

calls to make, deals to conclude. Work grounded him, kept him sane. Made him feel useful and alive.

Yet as he sat down at his desk and punched in the numbers on the telephone—it took a damnably long time—he found he couldn't concentrate. All he could think about was Zoe lying upstairs, her golden hair spread across the pillow like some kind of Rapunzel, the scent of rose water perfuming the air. What was she thinking? Was she glad to be here? Would she be bored? Would she discover the truth of him, even before he told her?

Suppressing a groan of frustration, Max forced his mind back to the telephone conversation that would conclude a multimillion-dollar deal—a deal he'd worked months for, that now felt as empty as his own bleak heart.

Zoe wandered up the marble steps, her fingers trailing along the wrought-iron railing, to the main floor of bedrooms. She peeked in a few rooms; each one was spectacularly decorated, the nautical colours perfect for the beach house and its many views of the sound.

Which bedroom was Max's? They were all anonymous guest rooms, and Zoe had the unwelcome feeling that Max would choose a bedroom as far from hers as he could. Perhaps that's why he'd asked her to pick one first.

Whatever had transpired between them before seemed well and truly gone.

Zoe finally picked a room in the centre of the house, its bay window overlooking the beach. She prowled around restlessly for a few minutes, examining the array of little soaps and shampoos in the en-suite bathroom, uselessly straightening a towel, glancing disinterestedly at the row of glossy paperbacks on the bookcase. Finally, for lack of anything else to do, she stretched out on the king-size bed with its smooth navy sheets—sheets so similar to Max's back in New York—and after only a few moments she fell asleep.

When Zoe awoke the sun was slanting its long, mellow rays across the water, turning the sea's surface to burnished gold. The sky was cloudless and hazy, a few seagulls circling over the water. All around her the house seemed utterly still and empty and Zoe wondered where Max was, what he'd been doing. She must have slept for several hours. Her stomach growled, and she realised she was hungry. She hadn't eaten anything all day.

After a quick brush of her hair and teeth—she looked basically presentable, which seemed as much as she could hope for these days—she wandered downstairs, room after room empty and silent, lit only by the long, setting rays of the sun.

She found Max in the kitchen, a hymn to granite and stainless steel, standing at one of the counters, two foil containers in front of him. The pungent aroma of tikka masala wafted through the room, and Zoe's stomach growled again.

'You remembered,' she said, and heard the pleasure in her own voice.

Max looked up, turning his head so he wasn't quite looking at her; his face was unsmiling.

'Yes. Are you hungry?'

'Starved.' She hesitated, unsure how to gauge Max's mood, uncertain what the source of the sudden tension in the room was. Of course, there had always been a tension between them. Why should she expect anything different, just because he'd ordered her a takeaway, for heaven's sake? It was a moment's kindness, nothing more, perhaps not even that. 'Shall I get some plates?' she asked, injecting a bright note into her voice.

'Good idea. They're above the sink.'

Zoe busied herself with fetching plates and forks, and setting two places at the huge oak table in the breakfast nook of the kitchen. French doors led directly out onto a patio with a flagstone path leading to the beach, the water now lost in darkness.

Within a few minutes they were both sitting down at one end of the table, the kitchen huge and empty around them. Zoe took a bite of chicken and closed her eyes.

'Good?' Max asked, and she heard a hint of laughter in his voice.

'Heavenly. It's wonderful just to *enjoy* eating something for a change.' She opened her eyes, smiling ruefully. 'I didn't realise I took my health for granted until I started feeling so utterly unwell.' She took a piece of nan bread, dipping it in the sauce. 'At least it will pass.'

'Yes,' Max agreed after a tiny pause. 'It's only temporary.'

They both lapsed into silence, and Zoe thought Max looked even grimmer than before. 'So,' she finally said, determined to keep this awkward conversation going, 'I don't really know anything about you.' Max merely lifted one shoulder in what Zoe supposed was a shrug. 'Where did you grow up?'

'Connecticut.'

'Do you have any brothers or sisters?'

'Three sisters, older than me.'

Zoe smiled teasingly. 'You must have been dreadfully spoiled.'

Max paused, his head cocked to one side, considering the question. 'Not particularly,' he finally said, and Zoe resumed her one-way questioning. It wasn't so much a conversation, she supposed, as an interrogation.

'Did you have any pets?'

'Pets?' Max repeated in surprise, and arched an eyebrow.

'We had a family dog named Boots. She died when I was six.'

'That must have been hard.' His only answer was another shrug; Zoe pressed her lips together. 'Have you always been in business?'

'No.'

'What did you do before?'

A pause; Zoe wondered if she was finally getting somewhere. Learning about Max was like wandering in the dark, unsure of every step. 'I was in the air force.'

'Miltary?' Zoe said in surprise, even as she thought, *Of course*. Now she understood his sense of precision, the cool self-control of his movements and reactions. 'For how long?'

Another pause. 'Two years. The air force paid for college. My second year I was called up to fight in the Gulf War. The first one.'

He spoke flatly, without any emotion, and it made Zoe wonder what he *wasn't* saying. 'You fought in the war?' she asked, even though he'd already said as much.

He nodded. 'I was a flight officer on an E-2 Hawkeye. We mainly did search-and-rescue missions.' He paused again. 'I left the air force after the war.' Another pause and he turned to stare out at the sea and darkness. 'I was honourably discharged.'

'You were wounded?' Zoe whispered.

'Our plane went down.' He pushed his plate away, the movement restless. 'Now it's my turn to ask some questions.'

'All right,' Zoe agreed, even though she longed to ask more. Know more. 'Go ahead.'

'Why did you come to New York?'

She swallowed, struggling not to avert her eyes. 'I needed a change of scene,' she finally said, keeping her voice light.

'Why?'

She swallowed again, a flush rising from her throat to stain her cheeks. She wanted to dissemble, yet she knew she couldn't. Honesty had to start somewhere. 'You remember that Internet search you did?' She toyed with her fork, her eyes on her plate. 'Well, in England the press was about a hundred times worse than that. Reporters on the lawn, ringing up all hours. It was ghastly.' She wasn't about to go into the truth of her father, the rejection she'd received in New York.

Max didn't say anything for a moment. 'So you left to escape the press?' he said, and Zoe knew he didn't buy it. He didn't believe her. And why should he? As much as she'd wanted to be honest, she hadn't been, not even with herself.

'No, I left to escape myself.' The words surprised her even though she knew they were true. 'When I found out I wasn't my father's…Oscar's child—I wasn't a Balfour—it was like I'd lost an arm or a leg or—'

'Your sight?' Max filled in, and Zoe nodded.

'Yes. An essential part of me. And I didn't know who I was, who I could be, without it.' She gave her head a little shake. 'I still don't.' She lapsed into silence, both wanting and dreading Max to say something, equally afraid of his judgement or pity.

'Well, how old are you? Twenty-four, twenty-five?'

'Twenty-six.'

'You have plenty of time to figure out those questions.' He pushed back from the table, suddenly seeming caged, restless. 'I'm thirty-eight.'

'And you've served in a war and have a multimillion-dollar business,' Zoe returned a bit wryly. 'What do you have to figure out? I'm sure you know exactly who you are.'

Max let out a low laugh; there was something almost

grim in the sound. 'Don't be so sure,' he said, and Zoe stared at him in surprise. 'Anyway,' he continued, his voice softening a bit, 'you'll get there. You're stronger than you think.'

It was exactly what her father had said. Yet Zoe couldn't quite believe it. She wanted to, desperately, but she didn't feel strong. At all.

'How about some other questions?' she asked lightly, taking another bite of chicken. She didn't want to talk about herself any more. 'Like what's your favourite colour?'

Max flashed her a brief smile, although there was something sad about the curve of his mouth. 'All of them,' he said quietly. He turned his face away from her, and Zoe thought she heard him sigh, a tiny sound of loss and even despair. 'All of them,' he repeated, speaking so softly she almost didn't catch the words.

They ate the rest of the meal in near silence, and afterwards Max left for the sanctum of his study, citing work as an excuse, Zoe thought a bit bitterly, not to spend any time with her. Why had he invited her at all? Every time she felt as if she were getting close, Max pulled away again. Was he regretting his decision to invite her, perhaps even his decision to be involved in his baby's life? In her life?

The thought terrified her, and she was so tired of being afraid. She wandered around downstairs, examining each spectacular room before settling in the living room with a book. She wasn't particularly interested in reading, but she hoped that if she stayed downstairs Max might stop and sit with her for a few moments at least.

He didn't. At ten o'clock, exhausted despite her long nap, Zoe shelved her unread book and headed upstairs, feeling like the lone guest at an all-too-exclusive hotel.

She fell asleep only to wake suddenly, in the middle of the night, the moon sending silver rays across the floor of her bedroom. She could hear the gentle shushing of the tide outside her window, but something else had woken her—she felt the echo of it still reverberating through her tense body.

A sob.

She heard it again, that muffled cry, and wondered who on earth could be making such a sound. Was a child lost outside at this time of night? Was there someone here Max hadn't told her about?

She swung herself out of bed, groping in the dark, walking instinctively towards that faint, intermittent sound. It was, she realised, coming from inside the house. She tiptoed down the darkened hallway past door after closed door, until she came to the last door on the corridor and paused.

The silence was unending, a thundering in her ears. Her own breathing was ragged, her heart racing. She pressed her hands against the door, spreading her fingers wide against the cool wood. Then the sound came again, a ragged breath, as if someone were in pain. And it was coming from behind the door she touched.

Without even thinking about what she was doing, or considering its possible ramifications, Zoe quietly pushed with her hand, and the door swung inwards. She stepped inside the room.

There, in a spill of silver moonlight, lay Max. He was in bed, the sheets twisted about his bare body, his eyes clenched closed. He was asleep, and that sound—that sob—was coming from him.

'Max…?' Zoe whispered, no more than an exhalation of breath, but Max didn't hear her. He was dreaming…if such an expression of emotional agony could be considered dreaming. He looked as if he were caught in the throes of a terrible nightmare; it held him in its grasping jaws and wouldn't let go.

Zoe stepped closer. 'Max,' she said again, louder, but words had no effect. His fingers clenched on his sheets and he shook his head as if to ward off some great danger, helpless against its encroaching power.

'Max…' Zoe knelt on the bed, the sheets slippery under her knees, and touched his forehead, smoothing back his dampened hair. She longed to take this burden from him, ached with the need to comfort him, to give him solace. He thrashed against the pillows once more, and her heart twisted. She felt close to tears; they crowded under her lids and in her throat. 'Max…' She cupped his cheek with her palm, felt the flick of stubble against her fingers. 'Max…it's all right. It's all right… you're only sleeping.'

She leant closer to him, her hair falling forward to brush his face, and his hand came up to clutch hers, his grip like a vice, so her hand remained pressed against his cheek, and she was powerless to move. His eyes opened and he stared at her with a sudden, wild desperation.

'You're all right? You're all right?' he demanded, his voice harsh and raw.

Startled, and a little bit afraid, Zoe stammered, 'Y-yes, Max, I'm fine.'

His hand still clutched hers, nearly crushing her fingers. He stared at her for a long moment, and Zoe wondered if he was even seeing her. There was a strange and terrible look in his eyes, as if he were still caught in the nightmare.

Then he relaxed, his face softening, his grip loosening. Zoe began to pull back, but to her surprise Max pulled her to him, hauling her against his body and wrapping his arms around her in a way he never had before, as if he would take her into himself, fuse their bodies in one seamless joining. She snuggled against his shoulder, their bodies pressed together, joined at every joint, amazed at how well they fit together, hard against soft, large against small.

She looked up at him; his eyes were closed once more, but not in the grimace of pain they had been a moment ago. His face had relaxed, softened, and Zoe felt a little ripple of gratitude pass through her. Her own body relaxed.

Then Max opened his eyes and looked down at her for an endless moment, their gazes locked, before he lowered his head and claimed her mouth in a kiss so achingly sweet Zoe nearly wept. Her hands came up and bunched on the sleek, smooth muscle of his shoulders and she pressed herself even closer to him, wanting to touch him, feel him, even be a part of him.

Finally he released her, leaving her spinning, joyful and yet also bereft. Then he gathered her in his arms once more, his chin resting on her head.

'Stay with me,' he murmured. 'Don't leave me alone.'

'I won't,' Zoe whispered. There was no chance of that. She didn't want to leave him; she didn't want to be alone herself. There was, Zoe realised, no place she'd rather be than in Max's arms.

Still, she couldn't even be sure how aware Max was of his actions, or even how awake he was. Had he *meant* to kiss her? Yet even so, she didn't move, didn't want to break this new bond, fragile and wonderful, between them.

Max sighed, the soft sound one of relaxation and contentment. 'You smell like roses,' he murmured against her hair, and Zoe's heart turned over, only to still suddenly—horribly—when he added, 'Diane.'

CHAPTER SEVEN

MAX woke slowly, blinking the world into its blurry focus, but for once it didn't matter. He didn't mind the loss of his sight. He felt the sunlight warm on his face, could see its yellow glow flooding his bedroom—and his heart— with light.

He still felt a sleepy languor in his limbs, a contentment throughout his body that was so strange, so unfamiliar, he hardly recognised what it was. And why he felt it.

Zoe.

She'd come last night, here, to his bedroom. She'd lain in his arms; she'd *fit*. And he'd let her stay, he'd wanted her to stay. It had been good.

Even as his heart acknowledged this fact, his mind protested. *She saw you weak… helpless…unmanned.*

He closed his eyes against the light.

He couldn't remember more than a few fragments of the night before: the softness of her hair, the scent of roses, the gentle sweetness of her touch. When she'd lain in his arms, the old nightmare, the mocking voices and anguished screams, receded, as did his own father's censorious voice:

You have to let it go, Max. If you're going to be a soldier, a man, then you have to let it go.

He'd never let it go. He carried it with him to this day, the shame and the pain and the regret, and worse, the feeling of utter helplessness. He never wanted to feel that way again, couldn't bear the thought of Zoe seeing him like that....

Couldn't bear the thought of letting *her* down, failing again as he had before.

And yet. And yet she had seen him weak last night—a little bit, at least—and she hadn't left. It was—strangely, stupidly—only then that Max realised his arms were empty. He was the only one in bed.

Zoe was gone.

He fought back the sudden wave of loss and fear and swung himself out of bed. He jerked on his clothes; he'd learned to leave them folded by the side of the bed so he wouldn't have to sort and scramble through myriad unrecognisable garments.

Dressed in jeans and a loose button-down shirt, he walked through the house, hearing and feeling the mocking silence all around him. Where was she? Had she left? He went into every room, his ears and even his heart attuned to the tiniest movement, waiting for Zoe to say something, reveal her hiding place. To find him.

Why had she left?

Desperation gave way to annoyance and even anger. Had she actually gone without telling him? Had he repelled and disgusted her so much last night with his weakness, like a child who needed to be comforted because of a silly dream, that she'd *fled*? Shame burned, harsh as acid, inside him, corroding his courage and the sweet memory of Zoe next to him.

Alone in the centre of the kitchen, a fresh wave of fury pounding over him, he felt something. A flutter, a breeze, from the beach blowing over him, cool and sweet. He inhaled and smelled brine; the sliding glass doors that led to the beach must be open, and then he knew where Zoe was.

He hesitated, suddenly reluctant to venture out to the beach. He used to like the sea, the glint of sunlight on water, the freshness of the breeze. Now everything had changed. The thought of walking across such an unfamiliar landscape—he hadn't been to his beach house in more than a year, and then only for a few weeks—made him hesitate. Fear.

It was that little spasm of fear that hardened his resolve. He would not let fear rule him; he was stronger than that. He could be.

He headed towards the doors that led to the dunes, and then to the sea.

Walking barefoot in the sand wasn't easy, but God knew he was used to it. The shifting sand made him lurch and stagger, and he felt the remembered metallic taste of fear on his tongue and in the back of his throat, could almost feel the sharp prod of a rifle in the small of his back, hear the jeering voices, and taste the sour stench of a gag in his mouth.

And the darkness. The unending darkness he feared so much.

It was so much like before, like his nightmare, he could hardly bear it. He hadn't had such a strong sense of memory swamp him before—at least while he was awake. Sweat broke out, cold and prickly, along his shoulder blades, and he bent over, his hands on his knees, breathing deeply, hating himself.

This had all happened nineteen years ago. Half his lifetime. And he was still crippled by it, especially now he was losing his sight.

By sheer force of will he kept walking, one foot in front of the other, until he crested the dune and he could smell and hear the sea. He wasn't in the desert; he was on the beach. His beach, and he knew, absolutely knew, that Zoe was right in front of him. Relief flooded through him, weakening his limbs with its sweetness.

He blinked in the glare of the brilliant sunshine, its brightness making it even harder than usual to discern any shapes. Yet even so, squinting, he could make out a small, seated form on the hard sand, the graceful curve of a shoulder and back.

Zoe.

He walked forward until he was only a few feet away from her, shoved his hands in the pockets of his trousers and waited. Questions crowded in his throat: *Why did you come to my room last night? What made you stay? What made you leave?*

Yet he didn't ask any of them. Couldn't. He was, he realised with stinging self-contempt, afraid of the answers. So he stood there, listening to the seagulls call out with their mournful cries, imagined them wheeling in graceful arcs against an azure sky. And waited for Zoe to speak.

Zoe felt Max behind her and found herself tensing with a confusing mix of hope, relief and fear. He'd come and found her, yet now he stood unmoving and unspeaking, and she had no idea what he was thinking. Feeling. Wondered if last night— as intimate in its own way as their other night together had been—had meant any more to him. Had it meant anything at all? She didn't know if he even remembered it.

'You're awake,' she said, turning to smile at him, shading her eyes as she kept her voice deliberately light.

'Yes.' The single word was terse, making Zoe tense all the more. She turned back to face the sound, its surface smooth and placid under the morning sun.

'It's beautiful out here. I watched the sun rise over the water. It turned everything to mother-of-pearl. Amazing.' She was babbling, Zoe realised, and she sounded utterly inane. Yet it had been amazing, and watching the sea cast in luminescence, the world slowly awaken to colour and light, had been surprisingly restorative. She'd felt, strangely, as if she had been awakening as well—her mind and body and heart opening up to possibility.

She'd felt that when she'd woken up next to Max that first morning, as if colour and light were flooding through her, restoring her senses. As if she was, once more, alive. She'd felt it again, an hour ago, when she'd seen him sleeping next to her. She'd touched his cheek, loving the feel of him. Then she'd remembered how he'd called her by someone else's name and she'd slipped out of bed.

'I used to love watching the sun rise,' Max said, and there was a strange note of longing in his voice that Zoe didn't understand.

'Used to?' she asked, her voice still light and even teasing. 'Not a morning person any more?'

He paused. 'Not a sunrise person.'

Zoe nodded even though she didn't really understand. 'Neither am I, to tell you the truth. I usually sleep in far past dawn.'

'Somehow that doesn't surprise me.' The faint note of humour took the sting out of his words, and he sat down next to her on the cool, hard sand, his body tantalisingly close to hers. She could feel his heat, even his strength, and she wished she could touch him. She wished she were brave and confident enough to lean into him, to ask him what he was thinking and perhaps even tell him how she felt.

I think I'm in love with you...with the glimpses of you I see, when you let me in like you did last night.

She pressed her lips together and stared out at the sea.

'I used to come here as a child,' he said quietly. He scooped up a handful of damp sand and let it trickle through his fingers. 'I loved it.'

Zoe turned to look at him, desperately curious. 'Does this place belong to your family?'

Max shook his head. 'No. We rented a little cottage closer to town. I had this place built five years ago. I wanted the light to fill every room, to see it no matter what time of day it was.'

Zoe couldn't help but notice how he spoke in the past tense, as if his life were over. And perhaps, in some strange way, it was. Max, she realised, didn't seem like the walking wounded; he seemed like the walking *dead*. Everything about him was closed, shut off from life, from love.

Why? What had happened to him to make him so utterly remote, the bleakness in his eyes chilling and yet so unfathomable?

Or was she simply imagining it all, as a way to explain his own past brutal rejection of her?

And yet, Zoe knew, it was that bleak sense of loss that had first drawn her to Max, for she felt it in herself. Her life— the life she'd known—was over. No matter what happened, she could never be a Balfour—the kind of Balfour she'd been before—and that gave her a certain grief...a grief she felt Max, in some strange way, shared. Felt.

And yet when they were together—when they'd danced, when he'd held her in his arms—she hadn't felt that grief. And she didn't think he'd felt it either.

For some reason now, the thought didn't give her hope. It made her sad.

'Who is Diane?' She had not meant to ask that question. She wanted to forget that Diane even existed, that Max had

said another woman's name while he held her in his arms,
the taste of her still on his lips. Yet the memory of that one
little word had tormented her all morning, a thousand
pointless questions echoing emptily inside her as she
watched the sun peek over the edge of the water and then
flood the world with light.

Next to her Max tensed. She watched him drop the last
few grains of sand and flatten his hand on the ground,
spreading his fingers wide, as if he were bracing himself.
'Why do you ask?'

'You—you said her name,' Zoe said quietly. She turned
her head, unable to look at him. 'You called me Diane last
night,' she elaborated, and tried to shrug as if it were all a
bit amusing. 'I couldn't help but wonder.'

Max let out a sigh, whether of exasperation or some
deeper, more painful emotion, Zoe couldn't tell. Neither
of them spoke for a long moment; the only sound was the
shushing of the tide and the cry of the gulls. 'She was a
flight surgeon, one of my crewmates on the Hawkeye
during the Gulf War.'

Zoe blinked. She hadn't been expecting that. A socialite, an old lover even, at worst, a fiancée. But a
crewmate? Yet then again, why not? Those two years
must have been powerful and traumatic for him; why
shouldn't he carry the pain of those memories even now?
She remembered how he'd cried in disbelief, 'You're all
right?' to her and she asked slowly, 'Did she die when
your plane went down?'

Max let out a ragged breath. 'No. But sometimes I
wish she did.'

Zoe blinked again. She wanted to ask what happened to
make him say such a terrible thing, but she was afraid of
the answer. She was afraid she might not have the strength

to hear it, to know what demons Max was battling even now. To know what she was up against. She wasn't strong enough, despite what her father—and Max—had said.

In any event, Max did not give her the chance. He rose from the ground in one fluid movement, reaching down a hand to help her up. Zoe took it, if only for the opportunity to touch him again. His hand was hard and strong as he pulled her to her feet and then let go.

'Come on,' he said and, surprising her once again, added, 'Let me make you breakfast.'

Zoe followed him into the kitchen and perched on a stool at the black granite island, watching as Max moved around the kitchen with his careful, deliberate actions. He opened the fridge and took out a dozen eggs, glancing back at her. 'I hope you like scrambled eggs?' he asked wryly. 'It's one of the few things I know how to make.'

Zoe swallowed. She'd never been particularly fond of eggs, and the thought of eating one now made her queasy tummy take an unpleasant turn. Still, she was too touched by Max's willingness to cook for her—to even spend time with her—that she found herself smiling and saying brightly, 'Lovely.'

He got out a bowl, cracking six eggs into it one-handed and with a brisk efficiency Zoe couldn't help but admire. She could make coffee and tea and occasionally a decent piece of toast, and that was it.

He looked up, arching an eyebrow. 'Is coffee out? How about herbal tea?'

Zoe made a face. 'Wretched. I'll just have water.' She slipped off the stool to fetch herself a glass. She stood by the fridge and sipped her water, watching Max move around the kitchen with that precise military deliberation. He reached for a frying pan and put it on the sleek new range, pausing only slightly before he lit the gas and poured the frothy eggs into the pan.

This was all so normal, Zoe thought with a pang. So comfortable and *real*. She felt as if she could exist forever this way, enjoying the sun pouring through the French doors, the warmth of the tableau they created, with breakfast sizzling busily on the stove and Max standing there, surprisingly relaxed, in a half-buttoned shirt and jeans that emphasised his narrow waist and trim hips, his long, powerful legs encased in denim.

Zoe's belly turned over, tightening with desire as she remembered their kiss from last night. Max hadn't mentioned it. Had he remembered? Did she dare ask?

'I think the eggs are ready,' Max said, prodding them with a spatula. Zoe gave him another bright smile.

'Fabulous.' And amazingly, she actually didn't mind eating them; she liked it. Sitting at the table with Max in a pool of sunshine, she felt she could eat anything and enjoy it, for the moment was so pure, so perfect, so *possible*.

Max stretched his legs out and sipped his coffee while Zoe nursed her glass of water, wanting to make the moment last.

'So how did you make your millions, then?' she asked a bit pertly, and was gratified to see a flicker of a smile in return.

'I'm brilliant, of course,' he replied drily, and she let out a surprised laugh. 'And I will confess to a bit of luck. I made the right investment at the right time.'

'More than once, I should think.'

Max acknowledged her remark with a nod. 'A few times.'

'Do you like what you do?' It was an impulsive question, and Zoe watched as Max gazed almost somberly into his coffee mug.

'Yes,' he said after a long moment. 'I like it very

much.' He glanced up, his eyes narrowing slightly even though he smiled. 'And what about you, Zoe? Do you like what you do?'

Zoe smiled ruefully, keeping her voice light. 'You mean shopping and partying and spending my...my father's money?' She stumbled ever so slightly over the word.

'If that's what you do,' Max said after a moment. His head was cocked to one side, his expression alert and yet also approachable.

She took a sip of water, suddenly self-conscious, unprepared for honesty. 'It's what I've always done,' she finally said with a shrug, and even managed a little laugh. 'I suppose I can't imagine doing anything else.'

'You suppose?' Max repeated, one eyebrow arched. 'Aren't you sure?'

She looked up. 'I thought you said last night I had plenty of time to figure out what I want to do with my life.'

'A few questions could get you started,' Max returned with the hint of a smile. 'What did you want to be when you were a little girl? A ballerina?'

She laughed ruefully. 'No, I'm afraid I'm way too clumsy for that.'

'You weren't clumsy when we danced,' Max said quietly, and Zoe felt her heart contract as if a giant fist were squeezing it.

'No, but we were barely moving,' she said after a moment. 'That's about as much dancing as I can manage.' She kept her voice light even though her whole body hummed with the memory of that dance, and swayed instinctively as if she could still hear the lonely wail of the saxophone.

'Well, then,' Max asked. 'Did you want to be a rock star?'

Zoe rolled her glass, beaded with moisture, between her palms. 'When I was little, I wanted to be a scientist actually.'

Max raised his brows. 'A scientist? That's not what most little girls dream of.'

Zoe gave a reluctant little laugh. 'No, it isn't. But I loved science—I used to sit in my…my father's study and read his encyclopedias.' To her embarrassment, her throat was tight with an emotion she couldn't even name. Somehow she made herself continue. 'I loved the entries about exotic plants. I used to memorise facts to tell my sisters at the dinner table.' She paused. 'They thought I was making it up.'

'Why would they think that?' Max asked softly.

Zoe shrugged. 'I'm not very bright. I barely scraped through my GCSEs, to tell you the truth. University was quite beyond me.' She turned away, her cheeks flushing with the remembered shame, as well as the new humiliation of Max knowing. She didn't like to admit she'd as good as failed out of school—and an exclusive boarding school at that! She still remembered her science teacher saying kindly, 'Some girls aren't meant for university, Zoe. You have other talents…'

And so she did. She was *particularly* talented at having a good time.

'I'm sorry,' Max said quietly. 'It hurts to have a child-hood dream taken away.'

He sounded as if he spoke from experience, and it made Zoe curious. 'What about you? What did you want to be when you grew up?'

'A soldier,' Max said, and his voice sounded a bit flat. 'Always a soldier.'

'And you were as good as, in the air force.'

'I discovered the beauty of flying when I was fourteen,' Max admitted. A smile flickered across his face, lighten-ing the moment. 'My friend's father took us out in his little biplane.' His voice sounded faraway and wistful, lost in memory. 'It was magical, soaring above the clouds, away from everything. I didn't want to ever come down.'

Away from everything... What had Max been escaping? Zoe wondered. His description of flying reminded her of her own escape of choice, into the books in her father's study. And then later, when her form of escape had been the endless social circuit. When you were so busy having a good time, you didn't have to think. She'd hidden from her self—from her *lack* of self—for years.

The realisation shocked her. She knew she'd been running away ever since the news of her birth broke; she hadn't realised until now that she'd been running long before that. Running from disappointment, from fear, from a sense of failure that she hadn't seemed to turn out the way she'd wanted to. Meant to. That little girl who curled up in her father's armchair and dreamed about discovering things...knowing things— Where had she gone? And, Zoe wondered sadly, could she get her back?

'Flying sounds wonderful,' she said quietly. 'Do you think you'll fly again?'

'No.' This was said with such matter-of-fact certainty that Zoe sat back, a little startled.

'Never?'

'No. Never.' They both fell into silence, and then Max leant forward, a look of bleak determination on his face, harshening his features. Zoe's breath dried in her throat. She knew instinctively that they were both poised on a new threshold, that Max was about to say something...tell her something. The knowledge of it crackled in the air and she felt a thrill of trepidation, a tremor of fear, at what he might say. The look on his face heralded nothing good. 'Zoe...'

'Yes?' she whispered after a long moment when Max

didn't speak, even though his whole body was tense, as hers was, with expectation.

'I need to tell you…' He stopped, and a look of uncertainty passed over his face like a shadow before it was replaced by a grim determination. He reached for her hand, and they remained silent, sitting, joined by their fingers. Even as she drew comfort from his touch, a wave of dread was rolling through her.

'Max…?' Zoe whispered, and heard a wobble of uncertainty in her own voice. What was Max going to say? Zoe was suddenly startled by a shaft of fearful realisation that, whatever it was, it could change everything. And not in a way she wanted or was ready for. Without even considering what she was doing—or its consequences—she gave a light little laugh, the sound like the striking of crystal. 'Max, you look positively grim. Surely it can't be that bad?' She smiled, tilting her head to one side, and for a moment Max looked as if he'd been struck, as if she'd somehow hurt him. And Zoe knew she had; she'd defused the tension of the moment because it had been too much for her, and kept Max from saying whatever terrible thing he'd been going to say.

A look of almost relief softened his features and darkened his eyes, and he shook his head. 'No,' he said quietly, rising from the table. 'It's nothing. Nothing at all.'

Zoe watched him walk away, regret swamping her. She was so weak, she thought savagely, and afraid. Her father was wrong; she *wasn't* strong. As much as she sought Max's confidences, wanted to know his heart, she also feared she wasn't strong enough to bear up under yet another rejection.

'I need to work,' Max said, pausing by the doorway, and Zoe didn't think she was imagining the bleak note in his voice.

'Fine,' she'd said as brightly as ever. 'I'll do the washing up since you made the breakfast.'

Max paused. 'Thank you,' he said finally, and walked stiffly from the kitchen.

Disconsolately Zoe gazed at the dirty plates and cups and wondered how, when only moments before she'd felt so wonderful, she now felt so utterly flat.

'You want to what?' Max's fingers stilled on the handle of his telephone. He'd just been about to make a call; he did all his business by phone these days, using the radio and the voice-activated software on his computer to keep him up to date and fully functional. He dropped his hand and sat back in his chair, narrowing his eyes and tilting his head so he could see as much of Zoe as possible.

She stood in the doorway of his study, wearing something floaty and pink, her hair a blonde cloud around her face. He couldn't tell much more, but even so his gut clenched with an unexpected spasm of desire and he remembered the taste and touch of her last night—how her lips had felt against his, so soft and sweetly pliant, her body curling naturally into his.

Max forced the memories away. Whatever had happened last night, this morning had tainted it, destroyed any sense of hope Max had been nurturing that he and Zoe could have something. Build something together. The way she'd shied away from even the possibility of truth had hammered home the realisation of who she was. Who he was.

'I want to go into town.' Her voice was light, bright and airy. 'See a bit of this place. Or were you planning on keeping me shut up here while you beavered away in your study?'

'We've been here one day,' Max said, an edge to his voice. 'I hardly think you're shut up.'

He felt her shrug, heard the slide of fabric against skin. 'Still, Max, if we're going to get to know each other…' She trailed off, whether in innuendo or uncertainty Max couldn't say. 'Find a way forward…' she finished quietly, her voice sounding small.

Max looked away. *Was* there a way forward? He'd felt hope this morning, felt a freedom in knowing Zoe had seen him in his weakness and had not turned away. Yet still, they hadn't spoken of that night—both of them were complicit in the lie, acting as if it hadn't happened at all.

And it might as well have not happened, for the despair he felt now, as he squinted to see and wondered how on earth he could tell her the truth. The truth terrified him; what would it do to Zoe?

He'd tried to tell her this morning; he'd started to, at least. Then he'd seen her false smile, heard that crystalline laugh and knew in his gut she didn't want to hear. She wasn't ready. And why should she be? They didn't know each other well enough to have their relationship—if they even had one—tested so severely. What could a woman like Zoe, a woman so clearly used to the finer, *fun* things in life, do with a man like him? She'd been determined to have him involved in their child's life; would she want as much when she learned what he was and how little he was capable of?

She wouldn't have a choice.

He would not allow her to deny him his child.

His own childhood had been stark and hard enough. He wanted more for his own son or daughter. He wanted to give more. And yet even so, he wondered how on earth they could find that way forward. The thought of attempting some half-life with a woman who could only pity him made both rage and hurt boil up inside him.

Never.

Max swallowed and forced his gaze back to Zoe. He heard a sigh, a tiny, breathy sound, one of impatience and perhaps even sorrow.

'You want to go to town,' he said slowly.

'Yes.'

Max tapped a pen against the burnished wood surface of his desk. Scrambling eggs this morning had been hard enough. He'd acted on instinct, simple movements, yet so achingly, agonisingly difficult. His body had been taut, his nerves frayed by the unfamiliarity of the tasks, the complexity of such simple procedures. He'd wanted to do something, to prove to Zoe and to himself that he was capable.

Of what? His mind mocked now. Making breakfast? And was that really going to impress Zoe, when the thought of walking through town, encountering all sorts of unexpected obstacles, people, *things*, terrified him? An uneven step, an open door? Who knew how he might reveal and humiliate himself?

'Well?' Zoe asked, and Max forced himself to smile.

'All right,' he said, rising from his desk. 'We can go to town.'

The village of East Hampton was quaint in a wealthy, intentional way; Zoe couldn't help but admire the trendy yet tasteful boutiques, the handcrafted wooden signs, the strategically placed coffee shops. Yet even so, as she walked along the pavement past shingled shops with their cloyingly quaint picket fences, tension reverberated through and radiated from her body. Since the limo had dropped them off in the centre of town, Max had been acting like a man being slowly and excruciatingly tortured.

He walked next to her, his posture stiff, every step a

military march. His face was blank, his eyes dark, his jaw so tight Zoe wondered if it might snap.

For heaven's sake, she thought in annoyance, was walking through town with her such an imposition? Max didn't look as if he was irritated or bored; he looked worse. He looked as if he was in *pain*.

Was he in pain? Zoe wondered. How hurt—how wounded—was he still from his accident? Was that what he'd been going to tell her this morning? She didn't know if she had the courage to ask the questions or, more importantly, to know the answers. Just like this morning, her mind shied away from such thoughts, and her own cowardice shamed her. How could she expect to have any kind of future with Max if she wasn't willing to face the truth, however hard it might be? And yet despite this ignorance, she still felt irritated—and hurt, perhaps unreasonably so— by his cold, stiff demeanour.

She found herself determinedly making up for his own stoic silence, chatting and even flirting with every male they came across, trying on outrageous hats and filmy wraps, batting her eyelashes and letting her perfect, cut-glass trill echo through shop after shop as Max stood stiffly by the door, unwilling to enter, looking as if he were suffering the ninth circle of hell.

Or maybe *she* was. She certainly wasn't enjoying herself, despite every indication she gave to the contrary. Zoe knew she was falling back on old tactics, her old self. She wanted to provoke a reaction from Max, childishly so. She needed to see—feel—something from him. She also knew that she fell back on these old habits because she didn't know how else to act. Who else to be? The realisation annoyed and shamed her. She wanted, she realised, to change. She wanted to recapture that curious little girl in the armchair; she wanted to discover her hidden strengths and talents.

What hidden strengths? Her mind mocked. She pulled off the broad straw hat with its trailing silk ribbons and replaced it on the hat stand with a dispirited sigh. Max stood in the doorway, his expression tense and even a little angry. Zoe felt like walking up to him and shaking him. Hard.

What about last night? she wanted to demand. What about when he held her in his arms, when he kissed her as if he loved her—or perhaps just the memory of another woman, of Diane. Had they been lovers? Zoe wondered disconsolately, knowing she had no real right even to be jealous. Had something happened to Diane that made Max the man he was now, a man who looked as if the best of life had already happened, and yet whose nights held terrible dreams—memories—of what had come before?

Was *that* what he'd been going to tell her?

As the afternoon wore on, Max wasn't willing—or interested—in playing her games, and no matter how outrageously Zoe acted—laying a hand on the arm of a young sales clerk who couldn't even be out of college, batting her eyelashes and tilting her head with coquettish charm as he stammered a reply to one of her ridiculous questions— Max's inscrutable expression didn't change, and he didn't talk to her any more than he had to as he ferried her from one place to another.

By the end of the afternoon, Zoe felt defeated, drained, and yet all the more determined to get something from this man. It was, she thought despondently, like squeezing blood from a stone.

Did Max Monroe even have any blood? Was he a flesh-and-blood human being with a heart? For he certainly gave a good impression of not having one.

Yet then Zoe remembered how he'd held her last night, how he'd asked her not to go, how they'd danced, and the sweet memory of it all made her want to cry.

Had she ruined any chance she had with this man this morning? Could she get it back?

She dropped an outrageously expensive scarf she'd been pretending to admire and without even disguising the weariness and sorrow in her voice, she said, 'Let's go back.'

And Max, she saw sadly, looked utterly relieved.

Back at the house he disappeared to his study, and Zoe was left alone. The sun was starting to set, light being leached from the sky, leaving it a colourless canvas hung above the sea.

Zoe made her way out to the beach, the sand cool and hard under her bare feet. She sat down on the shore, letting the water lap at her feet, too dispirited even to think, much less attempt to sort out the tangle of her feelings. She didn't know how long she sat there, staring blankly at the sea. It had grown dark, she realised, and a little cold. She thought of going back to the house, skulking through the empty rooms, looking for Max. And then what? Would they continue this awkward dance as they tried to navigate around all the unspoken words, regrets, memories?

Zoe didn't want to do it any more. She was tired of this, all of it—this uncertainty and fear and endless regret. She was, she realised with a surprising, wry little smile, tired of herself, and feeling sorry for herself.

She couldn't change Max. She couldn't make him feel things he wasn't ready to feel. She could only change herself, and she knew she wanted to. She was ready to. Zoe took a deep breath, drawing her knees tight to her chest. The moon had risen in the sky, slim and silver. A few stars twinkled faintly.

She wasn't going to feel sorry for herself any more. She wasn't going to think about all the things she didn't have, all the things she'd lost. Instead she was going to think about what she did have: a family who loved her, a father who had faltered not even for a moment in his support of her, a baby nestled in her womb who she already loved. Deeply. And Max.

She was thankful for Max. She loved Max, Zoe acknowledged with a dawning sense of rightness, even as the realisation shocked her. She loved him; there was no possibility, no maybe, about it. It was good, strong and true. She loved the man who held her in his arms, who needed her. The man who made her laugh over a plate of eggs, who danced with her, swaying softly to the music. Was it possible to love someone so quickly, so utterly? Could she trust her own feelings? More importantly, Zoe thought with a wave of trepidation, could she tell them to Max?

There was only one way to find out.

Max buried himself in work all afternoon, eager to occupy his mind and distance himself from the debacle of that afternoon. Going into town with Zoe had, he realised, confirmed every fear and suspicion about their possible union.

Impossible.

He could never give Zoe what she wanted.

He'd barely managed walking around town for a single afternoon; the entire affair had been an exercise in endurance, as gruelling as any challenge he'd faced in the air force. He hadn't realised just how much of his sight had already gone until he'd been thrust into an unfamiliar terrain, the sidewalk pavement uneven under his feet, each ritzy little boutique a foreign landscape with a hundred different obstacles to navigate.

He knew he should just tell Zoe; it was absurd to hide such a thing from her. Childish, even, as if he were a frightened little boy who had done something wrong and was vainly attempting to hide the implicating evidence.

He could have told her this morning, as he'd meant to; at the last moment his courage had failed him, and perhaps hers had as well, for he didn't think he'd imagined the flicker of relief in her eyes.

He could have told her about his past. She'd asked about Diane, and he had skirted away from the truth, not wanting to relive that terrible month, even though those days still haunted his dreams and made him wake up in a sweat of fear and regret.

He hadn't told her about the desperate cries he'd heard—and still heard—while he'd lain, gagged and blindfolded, utterly immobile.

The same immobility seemed poised to claim him now, for he surely felt as trapped, as tortured, as he had for the endless month he'd been held hostage.

CHAPTER EIGHT

'A PARTY?' Zoe looked up from the paperback she'd been half-heartedly attempting to read. She'd managed a page. 'What party?'

Max, still standing in the doorway of the cosy library where she'd holed up for the morning, shrugged one shoulder. 'An associate is having a party at his beach house. Some clients of mine will be attending, and I need to make an appearance.' Zoe didn't reply, and he continued, an edge to his voice, 'Besides, I thought you'd enjoy such a thing.'

'Did you?' Zoe asked quietly. Once, she would have. Once, she would have liked nothing more. She would have been bored without entertainment, attention and laughter. Yet now as she sat curled in the huge leather armchair that reminded her with a shaft of pain of Balfour Manor—and her father—she knew she wasn't that girl any more. She didn't want a party; she wanted Max. She wanted him to look at her and explain who Diane was, and why he had such terrible dreams. She wanted to ask him what he'd been going to say, and she wanted to tell him she was ready to hear. She wanted to tell him she loved him.

Yet ever since her self-revelation last night, she had not managed to find the opportunity. Max had been as closed up as a box, his tone and face forbidding. Nothing about him encouraged her to say much of anything, much less bare her heart.

She was, Zoe knew with stab of self-loathing, still afraid.

'Zoe?' Max asked, the edge to his voice more pronounced, sharp and bitter. 'Don't you want to go?'

She glanced away from the window and the view of the sun high in an azure sky. Max's face was half cast in shadow, despite the early hour of the day.

Too much darkness, Zoe thought with a sorrowful weariness. Too many unspoken questions and regrets. *Hopes.* And she didn't know how—or if she had the strength—to break the cycle. She found a bright smile and pinned it on. 'I'd like nothing better,' she said, and laughed, the cutglass trill seeming to echo through the empty rooms.

The sun was just starting to set, sending lavender streaks across the sky and glazing the surface of the sound in violet, as they set out for the party.

Zoe had managed to find a dress that still fit; her clothes were becoming alarmingly tight. She wore a halter-style dress in cream silk shot through with gold thread, the material floating around her and ending a good six inches above her knee.

Max, Zoe noted sourly, had not noticed her dress, or the pains she'd taken with her hair or make-up. He made no comment at all. He'd simply jerked his head in something like a nod and walked stiffly to the waiting limo, his driver, Frank, attentive as always.

'So who is this associate of yours?' Zoe asked, fiddling a bit nervously with the heavy gold hoops at her ears. She took in Max's perfectly cut trousers, his blindingly white shirt open at the throat. He'd developed a bit of a tan, which made the contrast between his olive skin and the whitened line of livid flesh bisecting his face all the more obvious and startling. Funny, Zoe thought, how she'd come almost not to see the scar, the mark of unspoken suffering.

'Just someone I do business with. I'm buying his business actually.'

'He must not like that.'

Max shrugged. 'Tough.'

Even though Max was seated next to her and she could inhale the musk of his cologne— of him—he still felt impossibly remote, as remote as he ever had. More. The thought of telling him she loved him seemed impossible, ludicrous, and yet still the words seemed to rise straight from her heart to clog her throat. She actually opened her mouth—a tiny sound came out, something halfway to a moan, and Max turned sharply.

"Are you ill?"

Zoe swallowed a wild gurgle of laughter. *Yes*, she thought, *I must be. To think I love you…and you can barely look at me now.* Max arched an eyebrow, impatient, and she shook her head.

By the time they arrived at the beach house, its wide, shingled veranda strung with lights, Zoe felt brittle and ready to break. Max hadn't said a word the entire trip; he hadn't even looked at her. Zoe felt as if she were in his company on sufferance, and the pathetic dreams she'd cherished of building some kind of life together—of loving him—seemed utterly absurd.

She turned away from him, straightening a little as they walked into the party, tossing her hair over her shoulders. The first interested and appreciative glance was like a balm to her starved soul, and Zoe found herself instinctively— childishly perhaps—reacting to it, just as she had when they'd gone to the village. Recklessly she accepted a glass of wine and drained it in one defiant sip. Tonight, she decided savagely, she was going to have fun… like she always had.

She didn't have any fun at all. Even as she chatted and laughed and flirted her way across the room, working the party with an instinctive, inborn charm, she felt dead inside. She refused to look for Max, and yet her heart cried out, knowing he was near…and utterly oblivious.

Still, she persevered, her laughter taking on a ragged, desperate edge as she sought to lose herself in the party, in the woman she'd once been, and to forget Max's—and every other man's—rejection of her.

It didn't work. Even as she stood in the centre of the room, holding court with several young city types, she was conscious of Max in the corner, his expression closed, eyes flinty as he spoke with a business associate.

'What did you say your last name was again?' A young man, all fake tan and too-white teeth, smiled at her as he asked the seemingly innocuous question. Zoe's smile froze on her face, making her realise how utterly fake it was. *She* was.

She took a sip of sparkling water. 'I didn't actually,' she said sweetly. Was she imagining that hard glint in the man's eyes? She couldn't even remember his name, though they'd been supposedly laughing and chatting for the better part of an hour.

'Balfour, wasn't it?' he suggested pleasantly. 'You're one of the Balfour girls.' Zoe stilled, saying nothing, and he continued with only a touch of malice, 'Or are you?'

The others gathered around shifted both in interest and unease, sensing the ugly undercurrent of the conversation.

The man waited, his smile turning to a sneer, and out of

the corner of her eye Zoe saw Max slip from the room, out onto the veranda that led to the beach.

She felt the flush of humiliation on her face, the sting of it in her soul. And yet even so, as she saw Max leave, she realised she didn't really care at all. She smiled at the man, at everyone. 'I'm afraid I've forgotten your name,' she said sweetly, 'but I don't have the time to learn it. Excuse me.' Depositing her empty glass on a tray, she left the room in search of the one person who really mattered.

Outside a breeze was blowing from the sea, cooling Zoe's heated cheeks. She picked her way across the uneven sand before discarding her heels in impatience, and made her way on bare, silent feet to the shore where Max stood, staring out at the ruffled surface of the water, a few sail boats and yachts bobbing in the distance, no more than pin-pricks of lights relieving the darkness.

Her heart still pounded, and her cheeks felt hot from the abandoned conversation, the ugly innuendo. Her arms crept around her body in a vain attempt to ward off the chill that was coming not from the sea breeze but from inside herself.

There would always be people like that man in there, or Holly Mabberly, or whoever else saw her as no more than gossip fodder, vicious amusement. She realised in that moment that she no longer cared what they thought; she cared only about the man standing in front of her, his shoulders bowed from the weight he carried—a weight she didn't understand. Yet she wanted to, wanted to reach out to him and tell him she understood…she needed to understand. Wanted, finally, to tell him she loved him.

Yet even now, standing in the sand with the breeze blowing her hair into tangles, she was afraid. Afraid that Max would reject her, that she couldn't be enough. That he would only see Zoe, the shallow socialite, and not Zoe, the girl in the armchair. The real Zoe. The person she was, the person she could be.

You're stronger than you think.

She turned her unseeing gaze back to Max; he hadn't moved from the shore. His body was rigid, his head bowed, his whole position seeming strangely vulnerable. Slowly Zoe picked her way across the sand to be closer to him.

'Max?'

'You were having a good time in there,' Max remarked, his back still to her. His voice sounded terribly hard.

'Actually, I wasn't,' Zoe replied after a pause. 'I was just pretending I was.'

'You told me that the first night,' Max said. He shoved his hands into his pockets and tilted his head to stare at the sky, now riddled with stars. 'You told me you were bored, you were just better at pretending than I was.'

'I've always been good at pretending,' Zoe agreed quietly. She felt as if she'd been pretending her whole life. She was ready to stop. 'But I'm not sure I want to any more.'

'Don't you?' The question sounded bleak rather than barbed, and then Max let out a shuddering sigh that was half laugh, half sob.

In that moment Zoe knew this wasn't about her. This was about Max. Her fear fell away as she walked towards him, a man who was so clearly hurting. She could see the mental anguish in every taut, harsh line of his body. He didn't move even as she stood behind him, tentatively raised her arms to touch his shoulders; his shirt was damp with sea spray.

'Max,' she whispered, wanting the right words so desperately, yet unsure what they were. What he needed to hear. 'What is it?'

She thought he wouldn't answer. He was silent for so

long, unmoving, his body tense under her hands, although at least he did not shrug her touch away.

'I thought you didn't want to know,' he finally said, his voice so low Zoe almost didn't hear it. She realised with a chill just exactly what he was talking about. Yesterday morning, when she'd deflected the intensity of that moment in the kitchen, when he'd said her name in a way that both thrilled and frightened her. When she hadn't had the courage to hear what he might say. She still didn't know if she was brave enough, strong enough, but she wanted to be.

You're stronger than you think.

'What is it?' she asked again, her voice a whisper. She pulled on his shoulders, wanting to touch him, *reach* him, but he didn't move or respond, and she might as well have been trying to tear down a brick wall with her bare hands. It felt as painful, as futile. Then, just when she felt despair creep in, knowing she was failing to reach him, he turned around, slowly, reluctantly, so they were facing each other, eye to eye.

In the starlight Zoe could barely make out his face; the moonlight slid over his scar, shadowed his eyes and cheek-bones. Neither of them spoke, although she could hear the ragged tear of his breathing. Slowly, hesitantly, and yet with a growing certainty, she reached up to touch his face, her fingers brushing against the stubble, her thumb finding the fullness of his lip. She cupped his cheek with the palm of her hand as she had the other night, when he'd been racked by such a terrible dream. Its memory, Zoe thought, still held him now.

'Max...' she whispered, the word no more than a breath, yet she still meant it as both a plea and promise. She wanted to know; she wanted him to tell her. 'Tell me.'

He moved closer and brought his forehead to rest against hers, their faces close, their breath mingling. Her hands slid down his face, across his shoulders and found his; their fingers entwined.

A few strains of music could be heard from the open French doors, faint and haunting, and with a little laugh Max said, 'We could almost be dancing.'

Tears stung Zoe's eyes. She'd never felt so achingly close to someone before, and yet still so agonisingly far away. 'Then let's dance.'

He paused, his eyes closed. 'I told you I didn't dance.'

'You showed me you did,' Zoe whispered. 'Remember?'

Max gave a little shake of his head. 'This time I don't know the steps.'

She closed her eyes too and swayed her hips, stumbling a bit on the sand, her fingers still threaded with Max's. 'Neither do I. We can just make them up. Create a whole new dance.'

To her surprise—and joy—she felt Max swaying against her, with her. 'Do you think it would be any good?' he murmured against her hair.

'I think it would be wonderful,' Zoe whispered. Her throat was so tight it was hard to get the words out. She felt Max's fingers tighten on hers. They swayed to the strains of music for a few wonderful minutes, moving almost as one, the waves lapping at their feet and the darkness all around them. Then Max gave her fingers a final squeeze and stepped away so quickly that Zoe was left half stumbling in solitude.

'Max—'

'I'm blind, Zoe.'

Her mouth opened, but no words came out. Her mind was spinning, struggling to keep up. *Blind.* She stared at him, his face lit only by the moon, his expression so terribly bleak, and her heart ached. 'How—' she began, even though she barely knew what question to frame.

'Stargardt's disease. It's genetic, a gradual degeneration of the retina which leads to seriously impaired vision or, as will most likely be the case for me, complete blindness.' She still could only stare; there were too many questions, too many thoughts, and she knew by the rigidity of Max's stance that she had to speak carefully. 'I had no idea I had the disease until my accident,' Max continued in a dispassionate tone. 'I blacked out, you see—that's why I crashed my plane. Sudden blackouts can sometimes be a symptom of the disease, and my diagnosis was confirmed while I was in hospital a little over three months ago.'

Three months. He'd only known this for three *months*? No wonder he looked like a man whose life was over. He'd had so little time to adjust to such devastating news.

'Since then my vision has only gotten worse,' Max continued, and she heard the strain in his voice, felt the sorrow. 'I can hardly see anything at all, and the simplest tasks are difficult…impossible—' He broke off, took a deep breath and continued. 'Sometimes I catch a glimpse of something—your hair, or the green of your eyes. They're so very lovely.'

She felt a tear slide coldly down her cheek and tried to speak, but Max wouldn't let her. 'But really I can't see anything at all. Blurred shapes, patches of darkness, sometimes something out of the corner of my eye. Peripheral vision, apparently, is the last to go. Eventually—' he swallowed '—it will all be dark.' His voice throbbed with feeling and Zoe dashed at the tear on her face. She would not be weak. Not now, not when this was so important.

'Max—'

'So you see why I was reluctant to have a relationship with you. I'm not—and I never can be—the man you thought I was. The man you want and need me to be.'

'How do you know what I want?' Zoe asked, her tone raw, her throat aching. Everything was making terrible sense: his careful, deliberate movements, the look of uncertainty she'd seen flash across his features...why he hadn't looked at the ultrasound screen.

And hear it, he'd said about the galloping sound of their baby's heart. Now Zoe understood why that had been so precious.

Max arched an eyebrow in blatant scepticism. He was distancing himself; she could feel it. He was becoming remote because it was the only way to protect himself from pain, or the possibility of pain. She knew all about that. Max protected himself by withdrawing; she did it by diving into the fray, laughing and flirting and partying her way to forgetfulness. Neither method ever really worked. 'Are you saying,' he asked in a voice that was all too cold, 'that it doesn't matter?'

'Matter?' Zoe repeated incredulously. She blinked back the threat of tears and thought of how her own father had told her the circumstances of her birth hadn't mattered. But they did; she felt it deep inside. It mattered, and it also mattered what she did. How she responded. 'Of course it *matters*—'

Max took a step back on the sand, his expression turning terribly blank, and Zoe reached out with desperate, empty arms. She'd said the wrong thing—she could see it in his face—and she hadn't even realised, hadn't meant...

'Max, no—'

'I knew what kind of woman you were the moment you sidled up to me,' he said, each word deliberate, cutting, aiming to wound. 'A shallow socialite and an accomplished flirt. That was why I took you to bed—I didn't want to have to deal with the morning after, and I knew you wouldn't give me any trouble. That's all you wanted too, wasn't it? At least, at first.'

Zoe shook her head, refusing to listen, to believe. 'Don't—'

'But it's true, Zoe. Remember that Internet search? I found plenty of fodder. Scandal.'

Zoe felt the blood drain from her face. The spotlight had swung towards her, and she didn't like its penetrating glare. 'I'm sure you did,' she whispered.

'You have quite an interesting history,' he continued, and now there was no disguising the sneer. 'Failed out of school at sixteen. You were nearly expelled for sneaking out and partying with local boys.' Escapades she'd almost forgotten. Now they were thrown at her as judgements, and from the one person in the world she couldn't bear to know and say such things. 'And you continued that reputation in London, spending your daddy's money on having a good time— except he's not even your daddy, is he? As we both know.' This was stated with a cold matter-of-factness that left Zoe winded and gasping for air, as if she had been struck. 'Not,' Max finished with chilling precision, 'that any of it *matters*.'

'Why are you saying this?' she asked, her arms around herself, her back bent and shoulders hunched as if she'd been punched in the stomach. She felt as if she had, or, worse, stabbed in the heart.

'Because it's true.'

Zoe shook her head. 'No, Max—'

'You're denying it?' he asked incredulously, and Zoe gave a little, hiccupping laugh.

'No, I can't deny it. Everything you said is true.' She raised her head, met his contemptuous gaze. Perhaps he couldn't see her, but he could hear the truth in her voice. 'I came to New York to escape the gossip when the news of my birth broke. I told you that before. And before that I was everything you've said I was.' She gave another little laugh. 'I admit it, I haven't done much with my life. I haven't fought a war or started a business or made millions. I never even thought about doing anything until I learned the truth, that I'm not a Balfour. I'm not who I thought I was.'

'And that's so important to you?' Max asked, the question a sneer. 'Being a Balfour?'

'It was,' Zoe confessed quietly. 'It was everything to me. I felt like if I wasn't a Balfour, I didn't know who I was. But now—'

'I know who you are,' Max cut across her. His voice was icily calm, chilling Zoe to the heart, to the bone. 'You're a shallow, vacuous socialite who's been amusing herself with some pathetic dream of happy families.'

'No—' Zoe gasped, the word choked from her. She could hardly believe Max was saying these things; it hurt so much more than any newspaper's rubbish or acquaintance's sly remark.

'It's only a matter of time before you get bored,' Max finished with cutting clarity. 'Before you walk away and move on to the next amusement.'

'That's not fair—'

'Just true.'

She shook her head slowly. 'Why are you saying these things?'

'Because it's better to end this now,' Max said. 'Before anyone could get attached.'

'*Attached?*' Zoe repeated, her voice somewhere between a sob and a squawk. 'I was falling in love with you—'

'Well, then.' The curling of Max's lip wasn't a smile; it was too cold, too cruel, for that. 'It's a good thing you stopped.'

Zoe closed her eyes. She felt dizzy and sick, as if she'd been physically attacked. She *felt* attacked, violated, stripped bare. She could handle anyone else saying such terrible things about her, she realised; she expected it now. She'd endured it enough. She'd almost—almost—got over it. Yet coming from Max—Max, who she'd seen at his most vulnerable, and perhaps hers, who had let her hold him, who had held her—it hurt beyond bearing.

She lifted her head and drew in a deep, shuddering breath. 'It's a good thing I did,' she finally said, her voice ragged, and then she turned and walked away.

Max watched Zoe disappear into the darkness; it swallowed her up and when he breathed in he couldn't smell roses any more. He felt winded, stunned, his mind and heart both shattered.

It was better this way, he knew. Better to have her leave on his terms, rather than hers. Better to fail her now, rather than later, when he couldn't be what she wanted, or give her what she needed. It was easier now, even if it didn't feel like it.

It felt like hell.

He'd only experienced this futile rage and hopeless desperation once before, when he'd been blindfolded, gagged and tied, a prisoner of war listening to the screams of his comrades and unable even to move. Even though he had no such binds now, he still felt as powerless. Still—and always—a prisoner.

CHAPTER NINE

ZOE called a taxi from the party, climbing in and letting it speed her away, down the sandy track to Max's beach house, now no more than a darkened hulk huddled against the shore.

She would leave tomorrow, she decided, too numb to consider the practicalities, the implications. She'd hire a car, or a bus—something—to take her back to New York.

And then what?

She lay on her bed, her eyes closed, unable to think about the next step…if there even was a next step. Every word Max had said was like a knife wound, her mind and heart lacerated and throbbing with pain.

You're a shallow, vacuous socialite who's been amusing herself with some pathetic dream of happy families.

It hurt, she knew, because she believed him. He was right. She was shallow and frightened, afraid she'd fail herself. Fail Max. Fail their child. She'd run away when the rumours started over her birth; she'd deflected Max's confidences just yesterday; tonight she'd walked away from him because she'd been too hurt, too frightened, to fight.

Afraid. Always afraid and weak.

You're stronger than you think.

She rolled onto her side, drawing her knees up to her

chest, and wrapped her arms around her knees. *No, I'm not, Daddy,* she thought, her eyes closed. *I wish I was. I wish I was as strong as you believed me to be.*

It's only a matter of time before you get bored. A scathing indictment, and so unfair. So untrue. And yet Max had believed it, had said it with such chilling finality, and the fact that he believed it—thought so little of her—hurt her more than she knew it should. More than she should let it.

She'd believed Max might think more of her, because she'd thought more of him. She'd wondered about and hoped for something deeper, something hidden underneath his haughty demeanour, his chilling scorn. She'd seen it…felt it, tasted it, when she'd lain in his arms, when he'd let her comfort him, when he'd smiled, when they'd danced…

Why, then, had he driven her away with such terrible words, scathing indictments?

I'm not…the man you want and need me to be. Zoe opened her eyes, staring into the darkness, dry-eyed, her heart suddenly thudding in her ears. She'd known Max was distancing himself for his own protection; she'd felt it, yet she'd forgotten in the onslaught of personal accusations and judgements. She'd only been thinking about herself, and her own weakness.

Had Max been thinking about his? Was he driving her away because he was afraid she would leave him when she learned he was blind? Could he really think she was that shallow?

Or was he simply afraid…as she was?

Zoe knew she had to discover the truth. She had to know just why Max had driven her away like he did. She had to confront him.

The thought left her dry-mouthed with fear. She'd faced too many rejections, too many cold stares. She couldn't bear the thought of facing that again, of feeling so empty and alone again, with no choice but to walk away, humiliated and hurting. Yet what was the alternative? Life without Max—without the possibility of Max—was too bleak even to contemplate. It was no choice at all.

You're stronger than you think.

'I'm trying, Daddy,' she whispered, and slipped off her bed to search for Max.

The beach house was silent and silvered with moonlight, every room she slipped through quiet and empty. Zoe realised she didn't even know if Max had returned. Was he still at the party, forgetting his cares—forgetting her— with some socialite who really *was* as vacuous as he'd claimed she was?

Still, Zoe searched, slipping through the moonlit rooms on silent cat's feet, wanting only to find him, yet having no idea what she might say, what he might be willing to hear.

She finally found him in the first place she realised she should have looked—on the beach. She walked down the slatted wooden path between the dunes and saw Max near the shore. He was seated on the sand, his elbows braced on his knees, the waves lapping his feet. A thousand stars spangled the sky above him, and the surface of the sound glittered with their light. Zoe hesitated by the softly rolling dunes, unsure what to say.

She tried to imagine what Max must be feeling now; she wondered how much of the awesome star-filled sky he could see. Her heart twisted, not with pity, but with admiration. He was a brave man.

She walked forward, the sand cool under her feet, and sat down next to Max. Neither of them spoke for a long moment.

'I came to find you because I don't believe you meant all those things you said,' Zoe said quietly. Max didn't answer for a long moment, and she clasped her knees, her fingers digging into her palms as the silence went on and on—too long. Finally he spoke.

'Which things?' His voice was low, aching, and Zoe ached too.

'The bit about being a shallow, vacuous socialite who is going to get bored,' she reminded him. The words still hurt even though she tried to keep her voice light. 'Remember?'

'I remember.'

Zoe took a deep breath. This was harder than she thought; Max was giving her nothing. In the moonlit darkness his profile was hard, the line of his cheek and jaw harsh and unyielding. 'I won't, you know,' she said softly. 'I wouldn't, if you gave me the chance.' Still, Max said nothing and Zoe looked down at the sand, blinking hard. 'When you said those things, it hurt so much because—because I've always believed them about myself. I couldn't stand the thought of someone else believing them too—someone I loved.'

Max let out a ragged sound, something torn from him, something between a laugh and a sob. 'Don't, Zoe—'

'I have to,' she said simply. 'I'm trying to change, to be strong, and I'm not going to walk away without trying, Max. Without telling you everything.'

He shook his head. 'It will just make it harder.'

'Why?' She reached out a hand and touched his arm; his skin was warm and her fingers curled around his forearm, craving the touch. The connection, no matter how small. 'Why does it have to be hard? I love you, Max. I love the man I've come to know, when you let your guard down, when you stop trying to hold yourself apart—'

He shook his head again, more forcefully. *'Don't—'*

'And in those moments,' Zoe continued, her voice no more than a whisper, 'I believe you love me too.' She stopped, her hand still on his arm, and he didn't respond. She felt the tide shush around her feet, lapping over her toes, warm and salty, like tears. Her fingers tightened on his arm. 'Am I wrong?'

He just shook his head, his throat working, yet he didn't speak. Couldn't, Zoe thought, and she didn't know whether that gave her hope or sorrow. 'Tell me, Max,' she commanded, her voice soft yet strong. 'Tell me you don't love me. Tell me you meant all those things you said before, that I'm shallow and…and vacuous.' Her voice broke, just a little bit. This was so scary. This was more of a risk than she'd ever taken before, more of a risk than when she'd faced her biological father. This was her heart, life, love, everything, on the line. She waited, watching him; he didn't move.

Please don't turn away.

Max covered his face with his hands, his long, tapered fingers pressed against his temples. 'I can't,' he said in a voice so low Zoe almost didn't hear it. Her breath came out in a surprised, grateful rush, and Max dropped his hands to look at her, his expression so bleak it chilled and saddened her, even as hope bloomed deep inside. 'I can't, Zoe. But I wish I could.' Even as he said the words, his hand came to circle her wrist, pulling her towards him. Zoe went, unresisting, her head falling back as his lips met hers again and again, a desperate dance of their mouths, lips and tongues and teeth, a furious yet beautiful joining, both of them craving the connection.

'I should let you go,' he murmured against her mouth even as he kissed with a deep hunger that Zoe matched, her fingers threaded through his hair, her body moulding and melting into his as they fell onto the sand, their limbs entwined, their mouths meeting once more. 'I should let you let me go,' Max confessed raggedly in between kisses.

Zoe held his face in her hands, moving away a little bit to ask, her voice as ragged and breathless as his, *'Why?'*

Max let out a shuddering breath, and the wonderful moment—that moment of hope—was broken, shattered, so Zoe wished bitterly she hadn't asked such a question. He'd been *kissing* her; why had she asked any questions at all?

'Because there can never been anything between us.'

She touched her lips, swollen by his kisses, tasting of him. Her heart still raced and her body tingled. 'It's a little too late for that.'

Max shook his head. He rolled to a sitting position, and after a moment Zoe did too. Her clothing was rumpled and she could feel sandy grit in strange places—between her breasts, on her thighs. 'I mean it, Zoe. I can't give you the life you want. I can't be the husband you need.'

A shard of anger lodged inside her, splintering her soul. 'That's starting to sound like a tired—and rather convenient—refrain.'

Max swung his head around to stare at her, his eyes narrowed, and Zoe wondered if he was trying to see. His heart, she thought resentfully, was as blind as his eyes.

'What are you talking about?' he demanded.

'You don't know what I want, Max. You don't know what I need. And it's not up to you to decide whether you can or cannot give me those things.'

He sighed, the sound weary, and the anger drained out of the moment, leaving a far worse despair. 'Do you know what I hate about going blind?' he finally asked, and Zoe just shook her head, not willing even to hazard a guess. 'The sense of powerlessness.' Max scooped up some sand and let it trickle between his fingers. 'I felt that once before,

and I never thought I'd have to feel it again. The thought…'
He drew a breath, let it out. 'It terrifies me,' he finished so
softly Zoe wasn't even sure she'd heard him.

'When…?' she asked, her voice just as soft.

'When my plane was shot down in combat.' He gave a
little humourless laugh. 'Nineteen years ago, half a
lifetime, and I still can't get over it. Pathetic.'

'No—'

'We were captured,' Max cut across her useless denial.
'There were five of us. Four men, one woman. Jack, our
pilot, was in bad shape. He died en route to the holding
facility.' His face was averted from hers, and Zoe longed
to touch him. Reach him. 'The others were stable, but hurt.
More hurt than I was.' He paused. 'I was the healthiest, you
see. The most capable of giving answers.'

Zoe's whole body went cold. 'You mean—'

'It's standard,' he cut across any sympathy she might
have been about to offer. 'You're prepared for it. You expect
it. It's war after all.'

'But still—'

'There's no justification for abuse,' he said, as if he
were agreeing with her even though she hadn't said
anything. 'By anyone, any side. But I thought I was ready.'
Another pause; his head was still averted. 'I didn't think
I'd *break*.'

'Oh, Max.' It was all she could say. There were no
words, no useless expressions of sympathy or pity, she
could offer, no absolution she could give.

'They kept me blindfolded, you see,' he said quietly.
'They never took it off. I couldn't—' He paused, his throat
working, his eyes now closed. Sweat beaded his brow. 'I
couldn't stand it after awhile. I thought I might— I thought
I was—' He shook his head, let out a long, slow breath.

'Crazy. Insane. I felt like I didn't even know who I was any more. I couldn't remember what it was like to…see. Feel.' Zoe swallowed past the lump in her throat. She reached out and touched his arm again; to her relief and joy he didn't shrug her away. He didn't, she realised, seem aware of her touch at all. 'I didn't answer their questions. I stayed strong. I was *proud* of myself.' The sneer she'd once heard in his voice returned, his deepest scorn reserved for himself. 'Then they started on the others. I couldn't tell what they did. I only *heard*…'

Zoe remembered his words about Diane, and whether she'd died: *No. But sometimes I wish she did.* Now she was starting to understand.

'I told them everything,' Max said after a moment, his voice now flat and emotionless. 'I don't even remember half the things I said. I was gibbering like an idiot, tripping over myself to give them the information they needed. I would have sold my own mother.' He paused, turning to gaze unseeingly at the fathomless darkness, the stretch of ocean in front of them. 'I sold my own soul.'

'Then you aren't the first to feel you did so,' Zoe replied evenly. 'Plenty of men—and women—have reacted as you did, and no one blames them for it. Max, you were *tortured*—'

'Don't.' He held up one hand, his palm flat in front of her face, obscuring her view. The movement had the effect of both distancing and silencing her even though she was still touching him. 'Don't try to excuse or absolve me, Zoe. Trust me, plenty of people have tried. Doctors, nurses, comrades, friends. Even my crewmates. You know we all made it through, except Jack? They told me they understood. They said they would have done the same in my place. As though that makes it *better*.' He spat the word with contempt. 'It's why I left the air force. An honourable discharge, because of war wounds, but the reality is there was no honour in it at all. I couldn't hold my head up. I couldn't even stand to look in the mirror.'

Zoe wondered how much judgement and condemnation Max had poured on himself. More, she suspected, than anyone else had. Then she was proved wrong by his next words.

'My father saw my true colours. *Colour.* Yellow.' His mouth curled in a grim little smile. 'We haven't spoken since I left the air force. He fought in Vietnam. He was a POW too. *He* didn't—' He stopped and simply shook his head. Zoe didn't say anything; she couldn't speak. She simply kept touching him, her hand on his arm, faintly squeezing, offering him her silent comfort and compassion. 'So you see,' Max finally continued, his tone final, 'why we can't be together.'

Zoe's hand stilled on his arm. She felt as if a bucket of icy water had been poured over her head, drenching her frail hopes. 'That's a non sequitur if I've ever heard one.'

'I'm surprised you know the meaning of the word,' he threw back, his eyes glinting in the moonlight, but for once Zoe refused to rise to the barb, refused right now to let her own pain matter more than his.

'I'm not buying that, Max,' she said evenly. 'Not any of it. You're trying to drive me away now because that's how you protect yourself. You're afraid of getting hurt.'

'And now you're some kind of psychoanalyst?'

Zoe smiled sadly. 'No. Just speaking from experience. I've been afraid too.' She paused, her fingers warm against his skin. 'I'm still afraid.'

It was a long moment before Max spoke. When he did, the rage and desperation were gone, replaced only by a weary finality that alarmed Zoe more than anything that had come before. 'Zoe, the month I spent hostage—blind-folded—was the worst of my life. I thought I'd put it behind me when I left the air force. I spent all my time—all my thoughts—on building my business. I even started flying again. When I blacked out in the plane and crashed, it shocked me. There was the pain, of course, but it also brought back the memories of when we crashed during combat. And then the diagnosis—it was like I was reliving it all again. The crash followed by darkness. Blindness. And even now the thought of being completely blind—of losing all light like I did before, of being so *helpless*… It terrifies me.' He turned to gaze at her with bleak honesty. 'I never wanted to be in such a powerless position again. And I won't let anyone be hurt by it—by my own inabil-ity—again.' He stopped then, and stared out to sea, leaving Zoe caught between fury, despair and an entirely unrea-sonable desire to pull Max into her arms and kiss him senseless—senseless enough to forget all these so-called reasons that would keep him from her.

'I see,' she finally said, and to her credit her voice was calm. Mild, even. 'So your desire to protect me from this powerlessness of yours is what is motivating your lack of involvement in my life? Our child's life?' Max angled his head so he was glancing at her from the periphery of his vision, where he'd told her he could see best. He didn't speak. 'Is that why you brought me here to your beach house? To tell me you couldn't be involved?'

'I'd hoped—'

'Oh?' Zoe cut him off; fury was winning over despair. 'And what made you change your mind?'

'Everything,' Max said simply. 'Everything is hard.' He gave a little laugh. 'You want to talk about torture?'

'Not particularly—'

'Going into town with you. Every second was a living hell.'

'I'm sorry my company was so distressing,' Zoe said, her tone a mixture of sharpness and levity.

'I don't mean being with you—' Max explained impatiently.

'I know you don't. But it amounts to the same thing, doesn't it? Because you're going to let your damn self-pity keep you from trying to be happy. From letting us be happy.'

'I can't be a proper husband to you, Zoe!' The words came out in an anguished roar. 'I can't stand by and watch—or *not* watch, as the case may be—while something terrible happens. And something *will* happen. Sometime. Some day. I'll fail you. I'll fail our child. Do you think I can risk that? Live with that?'

'Am I a prisoner of an enemy army?' Zoe demanded. She flung her arms out. 'Am I tied, gagged? No. This is not a war, Max. You may be blind, but you're far from helpless.'

'There will be times…things I can't do—'

'And there are things I can't do,' she shot back. 'I already told you I can't cook.'

'Stop trivialising this!' Max's voice was low and furious. 'You may think you can handle it, Zoe. You may see yourself as some kind of damned Florence Nightingale, but it's simply not going to be like that. Day in, day out—are you prepared to live with the kind of life I'd have to—'

'What, live as a recluse? Does being blind mean you can't interact with society? Are you going to start hoarding newspapers and collecting cats too?'

'Stop it.' Max slashed a hand through the air.

'No, you stop it,' Zoe returned forcefully. 'Stop feeling so damned sorry for yourself, Max. I know the signs because I've lived them myself. After the newspapers ran the story of my birth—*When Blue Blood Turns Bad* and more—I was racked with self-pity. I didn't even realise it at the time—I was so wrapped up in it. Poor little Zoe, who never knew her mother. Poor Zoe, who never felt like she belonged. The dumb one, the non-twin, the orphan. I suppose I let it be an excuse for my less than exemplary behaviour through the years. I let it be the reason why I didn't even have a reason, why I've drifted through life without thinking about a greater purpose, a deeper design.'

Max opened his mouth, no doubt to utter some scathing retort, but Zoe wouldn't let him. She *needed* to say this. He needed to hear. 'And then when I fell pregnant, I almost—almost—let myself play the poor little victim once more. Then I realised that a baby is the best thing that's ever happened to me. Not because I want a fashion accessory, but because I've found a purpose. I want to love and shape this little life, guide her steps and give her strength. I want her to see my mistakes without making them herself. I want to be a mother,' Zoe finished simply. 'And mothers can't afford to sit around and pity themselves.' She paused, let her voice turn hard. 'And neither can fathers.'

'I am not—' Max began. He stopped abruptly. 'I can see how you might look at it that way, but it's a point of honour for me, Zoe. I failed someone—several people—before. Diane especially.'

'I'm sorry, Max,' Zoe said, and meant it. 'But you can't let a single episode in the past—as massive and life-altering as it was—define your entire existence. You can't let it ruin your future, Max. Our future.'

'We have no future,' Max replied flatly. 'We can't.'

Zoe stared at him. She felt like screaming, like stomping

her feet and pulling her hair and crying like a child. A proper temper tantrum, that's what she felt like having, the kind she hadn't experienced since she was three years old. Yet even as the urge came over her, it left suddenly and completely, left her feeling empty and flat. There would be no reasoning with Max. No arguing, no understanding. He'd set his course, set his face away from her, and Zoe knew—felt it deep in her bones, in her broken heart—that he would not change. She couldn't change him. She could, as she'd reminded herself only yesterday, change herself.

Slowly, her body aching, she rose from the cold sand. She stood behind him, observing the rigid lines of his body with a strange, new, dispassionate calm. 'Just one question,' she said, her voice as flat and emotionless as she now felt. 'Do you love me?'

He didn't answer. Zoe realised she hadn't even expected him to. She turned and walked back towards the house, away from Max. It wasn't until she reached the slatted wooden path stretching between the dunes that she heard his reply: *'Yes.'*

Max stayed out on the cold sand until the sky lightened with the sun's first pale rays. He could tell that much; the darkness faded to grey, to nothingness, a blank canvas.

He felt as blank as the sky, empty and leached of light, although perhaps that was merely a way of protecting himself. For underneath that comforting numbness was, he sensed, a deep well of terrible emotion he could not bear to plumb. Grief, pain, loss, hurt, fear, guilt. Too much to feel. Too much truth to acknowledge.

Zoe was right. He did feel sorry for himself, had been struggling with self-pity since he'd learned his diagnosis. God knew, he wanted to be stoic. Strong. Take it like a man, as his father had urged him too since he was six years old and struggling not to cry when their dog had died. Breaking under hostile questioning had been the last straw for his father; as a son, Max had proved an utter failure. A humiliation, a source of shame.

And he felt it himself. Perhaps that was why he wasn't willing to risk a life with Zoe; he couldn't bear her to be ashamed of him. To lose her because of his own weakness. It wasn't a point of honour at all; it was simply a matter of fear.

Zoe didn't see Max again. She stretched out on her bed and watched the sky lighten, the stars going out one by one as if snuffed by the heavens. Perhaps she slept; she wasn't sure. When the hour was finally late enough for her to call a taxi service and arrange her transport back to New York, she did so, her body leaden, her heart numb.

She took a taxi to East Hampton, and then a bus—the jitney, full of sunburned weekenders, laughing and chatting or else sleeping through their hangovers—back to Grand Central. From there she hopped a cab to the Balfour apartment, and she entered the cool, quiet sanctuary of its elegant rooms with something almost bordering on relief. It was the closest thing to an honest emotion that she'd felt since leaving Max the night before.

'You're back.' Lila, grey haired, dark eyed, with a faint exotic accent—Zoe wasn't sure where she was from and realised, to her shame, that she'd never bothered to ask—stood in the corridor that led to the kitchen and the servants' quarters. 'Where were you?'

'I spent the weekend in the Hamptons.' Had she only been there for three days? It seemed ludicrous, impossible. She felt completely transformed, as ancient as if she'd been gone years.

Lila nodded, somewhat stiffly, and Zoe could only imagine what the housekeeper thought. Zoe Balfour, bored with New York and partying it up somewhere else. She smiled tiredly. 'I think I need a bath and bed.' Lila nodded again and turned to go back to the kitchen. 'Lila,' Zoe asked suddenly, 'where do you go so often? My father mentioned something—are you visiting a relative?'

Clearly surprised, Lila turned around slowly, her eyebrows elegantly arched. 'My sister. She has cancer—she's in the hospital. I visit her twice a week. If it is too much—'

'No, no,' Zoe said quickly. 'I just wondered. I'm sorry. About your sister, I mean.' She paused, seeing the lines of worry on Lila's high forehead that she'd never bothered to notice before, the dark shadows in her eyes. 'It must be hard.'

Something flickered across Lila's face, surprise perhaps. 'Yes,' she agreed quietly, 'it is.'

Everyone had a story, Zoe thought as she turned towards the bedroom wing. Everyone had a sorrow.

'Before I forget,' Lila called, and Zoe stilled. 'A man came by. He left a letter. It's on the hall table.'

'Thank you,' Zoe murmured. She hurried towards the little gilt table where the post was usually left, her heart beating with fast, frantic beats. Had he come? Right from the beach house, beating her own slow journey on the bus, to see her—

She turned the heavy cream envelope over, ripped it open. Her heart did a curious flip-flop of disappointment and surprise when she read the brief message.

I would like for us to meet. Please call to arrange a time at your earliest convenience. T. Anderson.

Her father wanted to meet her? Why? Did she regret the way he'd sent her on her way before? Was at least one man in her life coming back to say sorry?

It mattered so much less than Max, and yet the message—the contact—gave Zoe a small amount of solace, a little hope. Perhaps at least this would be made right.

When she rang Thomas Anderson's offices, she was put straight through to his receptionist; she remembered the haughty, frosty-haired woman with a patina of glossy make-up all too well.

'Mr Anderson will see you four o'clock tomorrow,' she informed Zoe crisply, 'at the Collegiate Club on Fifty-fifth and Fifth Avenue. Do you know it?'

'No,' Zoe said, 'but I'm sure I can find it.'

The receptionist hung up.

It was a beautiful day, the sun bathing the city buildings in light, as Zoe walked down Fifth Avenue towards the meeting place. The trees on the edge of Central Park provided leafy shade for the cobblestone path that led down to Fifty-Ninth Street, the famed Plaza Hotel presiding over that well-known corner. She walked past the streams of tourists and the sidewalk sketch artists, one enterprising soul decked out in silver paint as a Statue of Liberty mime. She absorbed it all, realising that she'd come to love this city, its vibrant energy and its colourful canvas of people. It was a shame, she thought with a wry sorrow, that she no longer had a reason to stay.

The Collegiate Club was a prepossessing building with an ornate, Italianate-style facade. Inside it was all dark panelled wood and book-lined walls, the spacious rooms still managing, to Zoe, to feel stuffy.

She found her father in the library; he sat in a silk armchair, spectacles on the edge of his nose, reading a report. He looked up as she came into the room, ushered by a silent staff member who disappeared as quickly as he had arrived.

'Hello,' Zoe said. Her voice sounded small in the large
room; the heavy Turkish carpets and endless rows of books
absorbed all sound.

'I took the liberty of ordering us tea.'

'Thank you.'

She sat down across from him, on the edge of a
matching armchair. He put down his report.

'I'm sorry for the way I spoke to you when you came
to my office,' he said. His voice sounded formal and
slightly stilted. 'You shocked me, obviously. When my receptionist announced your name, I thought—hoped,
really—that it was mere coincidence that brought you. I
hadn't heard the reports.'

'No?' Zoe asked quietly. Her fingers curled around the
strap of the handbag she hadn't let go of. She stared at the
floor, the carpet a rich swirl of reds and yellows.

'No,' Anderson said heavily. 'But I've since seen some
of the…articles…and I'm sorry, for your sake. What
you've had to go through.'

Zoe lifted a shoulder in a silent shrug. Funny, but the
horror and humiliation of those days after the story broke
seemed nothing to the emptiness and heartbreak she felt now.

Anderson cleared his throat. 'It seems, however, that
you have a very supportive family back in England. A supportive father.' Zoe looked up, surprised by his choice of
words. The tea things had arrived, and the same staff
member set out porcelain cups and saucers, a rather im-
pressive-looking teapot.

'Would you like to pour?' her father asked awkwardly,
and Zoe almost reached for the pot. Then she stopped and
sat back in her chair.

'Why exactly did you ask me here?'

'I wanted to explain—'

'Explain what, exactly?' Zoe pressed. She felt strangely, remarkably calm, and when Thomas Anderson next spoke she wasn't even surprised.

'As much as I regret…what happened, this situation isn't…tenable.' He spoke the words haltingly, yet Zoe still had a feeling it was a rehearsed, and unpleasant, little speech.

'Tenable?' she prompted when he trailed off.

'I have a wife,' he said. He sounded apologetic. 'And children—'

'Yes, I saw their picture. Three. Four, if you count me.'

Something hardened in Anderson's features, and without another word he handed her the manila folder he'd been perusing when she arrived. 'I'd like you to sign this.'

Zoe flipped it over and scanned the officious-looking document. It was a waiver of sorts, a gag order to keep her from ever acknowledging they were related. In return she would be given two million dollars. She looked up, dry-eyed.

'Do you think I need money?'

'I don't know,' he replied evenly. 'Since you're not actually a Balfour—'

'I don't receive any money?' Zoe finished. 'Fair point.' She flipped the folder closed and held it out for him to take. After a moment he did so, reluctantly. 'I'm afraid I'm going to say no to your offer,' she told him. 'As tempting as it might have seemed to you, when you were putting it together. But thank you for proving to me that blood really doesn't matter.'

'Zoe—' It was the first time he'd said her name.

'But don't worry. You don't need a gag order to make sure I stay silent about you. I don't want anyone to know I'm related to such a selfish, cold-hearted bastard.'

Anderson coloured faintly. 'That's not completely fair—'

'Oh, only partly? Would it have killed you to acknowledge me in some way? To explain? Did you love my mother?'

He blinked. 'I knew her for one summer. We were both unhappy.'

'I see.' Zoe rose from the chair. Her legs felt damnably weak, but her voice still came out strong. 'Well, you were right about one point. I do have a family back at home, and they've been incredibly supportive. So has my father. My real one.' She gestured to the impressive tea set. 'I'll leave you to pour.'

[illegible faded text from previous page bleed-through]

CHAPTER TEN

SHE took a flight home to England the next day. For it was home, and it always would be, as much as she'd fought against it, out of hurt and pain and a fear—like Max—of rejection. She'd faced her demons, faced herself, and she wanted to be where she knew she would always be loved and accepted. The place where she could change and grow and become the woman she knew she was meant to be.

She had stopped by the pregnancy centre before she left, thanking Tiffany and the other volunteers for their time and support.

Tiffany hugged her goodbye. 'You seem to have sorted yourself out,' she said quietly.

'I'm afraid the father's still not involved.'

'You can only control yourself.'

Zoe nodded. 'True words.'

'Anyway,' Tiffany said, stepping back, 'you seem strong. Stronger than you did when you first found out.'

Zoe smiled. 'I am,' she said simply.

She hired a car at the airport, not wanting to call Balfour Manor for their driver to pick her up. She didn't want anyone to know she was coming. She wasn't sure why she wanted to keep her arrival as a surprise; perhaps because she wanted to see them in that unguarded moment when they first caught sight of her, perhaps because she wanted to be real.

She was done with pretending.

She turned through the familiar wrought-iron gates, the family motto, *Validus, Superbus quod Fidelis*, worked into the metal in elegant script. Ahead of her the lawns rolled out towards the estate in a velvety green scroll, the house with its imposing yet no less dear facade, the circular gravel drive and the Renaissance-style fountain. She pulled up in front of the front stone portico and killed the engine. The gravel crunched underfoot as she stepped out of the car, and to her surprise the double doors that served as the main entrance to the manor house opened almost at once. Tilly, the manor's former housekeeper, her father's former wife and an often-surrogate mother to Zoe, stood there.

'Zoe!' She wrapped her in a gentle, all-encompassing hug, leaving Zoe with no choice but to return the embrace, resting her head on Tilly's soft shoulder with gladness. 'I'm so glad you're back.'

'So am I.' Zoe pulled away a little bit. 'Where's Daddy?'

If Tilly noticed how Zoe referred to her father she gave no sign. She simply nodded and tilted her head towards the house. 'He's in the study.'

Zoe nodded and slipped from her arms, climbing the steps towards her home. Inside, the foyer was cool and dark, and as she stood in front of her father's study, the door only slightly ajar, she thought she caught a whiff of tobacco. Smiling, she knocked lightly.

'Tilly?' Her father sounded absorbed, slightly impatient, and Zoe knew he must have been reading. She pushed the door open.

'Hello, Daddy.'

Oscar looked up as she stood in the doorway. He didn't say anything, merely gazed and blinked rapidly. Then he smiled and rose from his chair, discarding the book he'd been so absorbed in with careless ease. 'Zoe. Zoe. I'm so very happy to see you, my child.'

He enveloped her in a hug just as Tilly had, and once again Zoe leant against him, her head on his shoulder.

'I'm happy to see you too.'

'You found what you were looking for?' Oscar murmured against her hair, and Zoe smiled.

'I think so,' she said, her voice muffled by his shoulder.

He pulled away, smiling, although concern pleated his brow. 'You look tired. And pale.'

'It was a long flight.' She wasn't quite ready to tell him—or anyone—about her pregnancy, although she wouldn't be surprised if Tilly guessed sooner or later.

'Are you sure that's all?'

'It's been a long journey,' Zoe said, and she knew her father took her double meaning.

'But you're all right?' he clarified, and Zoe nodded.

Even if her heart was broken… She would be all right. She was strong.

'Good.'

'I want to tell you I'm sorry,' Zoe said. Oscar raised his eyebrows. 'For everything.'

'Zoe, my dear, there is nothing you need apologise for.'

'There is,' Zoe said. 'I was so hurt when I realised I wasn't really a Balfour. But more than hurt, I was afraid.'

'Afraid of what?' Oscar asked softly.

'Afraid of being scorned. Humiliated. Treated differently.'

'Not by us?'

'By everyone. I put all my identity—all my meaning—

into being a Balfour. When I found out I wasn't one, I had to take a long, hard look at myself.'

Oscar smiled faintly. 'That's never easy.'

'Or pretty,' Zoe agreed. 'But I got through it. And I'm stronger for it.'

'You always were—'

'Stronger than I thought. Perhaps you were right.' Zoe smiled; her eyes were damp. 'Thank you,' she said softly, and Oscar briefly touched her cheek.

'Zoe, it is my deepest pleasure. You are my daughter. I love you.'

'I love you,' she returned, heartfelt, and then she left the study.

The manor was strangely empty— Bella and Olivia were both off, having their own adventures—and yet Zoe didn't mind. Silence, solitude, didn't scare her any more. She didn't mind being alone with herself, her thoughts. Even if those inevitably drifted to Max, imagining what he was doing—or not doing—how he felt, if he missed her.

A few days after her arrival, Zoe knew she needed to act. She was not going to let herself fall into a lifeless lethargy, for she knew all too well how that could lead to a contemplative and unhelpful sort of self-pity. Instead she took action. She enrolled in a night course in A-level biology, and then found her way to the nearest market town, where there was a small pregnancy centre off the high street.

She smiled at the grandmotherly type standing at a tired-looking photocopier in the front office.

'I'd like to volunteer.' She gestured to the machine. 'I'm good with those.'

The days turned into weeks, and even as Zoe occupied herself with school and volunteer work, she knew she'd have to tell her father—as well as the others—about her pregnancy. It would soon prove difficult to hide her condition; and while her nausea had finally abated, her stomach bore a new, not unpleasing roundness and her breasts had become heavy and full. Her father might not notice such things, but Tilly and any one of her sisters certainly would.

Despite her newfound resolve, the sense of peace she'd come to have about herself and who she was, she was still nervous to tell her father she was going to have a baby, and that the father was nowhere in sight.

In the end it was surprisingly easy. They were having dinner, just the two of them, in the huge dining room, and Zoe couldn't quite manage the French onion soup.

'You don't seem to have much appetite,' Oscar commented, a telling shrewdness in his eyes. His voice still remained gentle.

'No…' Zoe clenched her napkin in her lap. She took a breath and looked up, meeting her father's clear gaze directly. 'The truth is, Daddy, I'm pregnant.'

Oscar's expression didn't flicker. 'Someone in New York?' he surmised gently.

Zoe nodded. 'He's not—that is, I love him—but…he's not ready to be involved.' That was an understatement.

'Then he's a fool.' Oscar paused. 'You want to raise the baby? On your own?' Swallowing, Zoe nodded, and Oscar raised his glass. 'Then let us toast this precious little one.'

And Zoe raised her glass too.

'I'm not taking no for an answer.'

Max gritted his teeth even as he smiled reluctantly at his sister Allison's fierce determination. 'You might just have to.'

'I mean it, Max. You've been keeping yourself apart for too long. I won't have it any more. Lunch tomorrow at

Nobu at noon. Be there, or I'll drag you by the hair from that modern monstrosity you call a home.'

'Fine.' Max was tired of fighting. 'Noon, it is.' Amazingly, as he hung up the phone, he realised he was almost looking forward to it. It had been four endless, agonising weeks since Zoe had left—since he'd made her leave. A few discreet inquiries by his assistant told him she'd returned to England. The thought made him ache. She was well and truly gone…and it was his fault. He thought he'd been doing the right thing, the only thing, yet now he found himself wondering. Wishing. Had he simply been afraid, and used honour as his excuse? The thought was terrible and yet all too possible.

'You look like hell,' Allison told him as he sat across from her at one of the restaurant's best tables. Forty years old, impeccably turned out and a high-powered lawyer, it was a testament to her tenacity that Allison had only recently given up trying to manage him. He imagined he could see the burnished gleam of her hair and nails even though his vision was too blurred to take in much.

'I feel like hell,' he said, surprised by his own honesty.

'Max? Is everything all right?' Allison paused, uncharacteristically uncertain. 'I know the accident shook you up—'

Max took a breath. Zoe had taught him one thing, at long last: he couldn't live in fear. He couldn't live alone and apart either. 'Actually, it did more than that,' he said, and he proceeded to tell her the truth of his condition.

Afterwards Allison insisted on ordering a second bottle of wine. 'I need it even if you don't,' she said.

Max gave a glimmer of a smile. 'I think I need it too.' He waited until the wine was poured and he was taking a sip of Dutch courage before he added, 'That's not all. It's not even the worst.'

'What?' Allison exclaimed. 'What more could there be?'

Max smiled sadly. 'I met a woman.'

'That sounds like good news, very good news—'

'I made her leave.' He didn't mention the baby. He knew Allison's contempt would be complete and scathing.

'Why?' Allison didn't let him answer. 'Not because of some godforsaken misplaced sense of honour, Max? Because of your blindness? Tell me you didn't.'

'Something like that.' Allison groaned. Max tried to smile. 'It seemed like the right thing at the time, but now I wonder—' He stopped, his throat tight. Wondering was the worst. Wondering made him feel as if he'd thrown away the best—the only—chance of happiness with both hands.

'Where is she now?'

'England.'

Allison was silent for a moment. Max could almost hear the cogs in her brain turning over. 'Do you think she loves you?' she finally asked.

Max's throat had tightened so much he could barely get the words out. 'She told me she did.'

'Then the only question,' Allison said, leaning forward so Max could smell her citrusy perfume and hear her jewellery clink and jingle, 'is what the hell you're still doing here?'

It was one of those rare, perfect summer days, the roses in full bloom along the gravel drive, the sky a deep, pure blue. Zoe had taken a rug out to the front lawn to enjoy the sunshine, a paperback forgotten on her lap. She felt almost completely happy, until she remembered. Then she experienced that jagged, lightning streak of pain that made her realise her happiness—as solid and strong a thing as it seemed—was really as insubstantial as smoke. It had been a month since she'd seen Max on that cold, dark beach and he'd sent her away. Gazing down the long, empty drive shimmering under the sunlight, Zoe realised she'd been cherishing hopes—hopes she hadn't even acknowledged to herself—that Max would find her. Write. Call. *Something*.

Not this unending silence, not when she knew he loved her, when he knew she was carrying his baby. Was he really so determined? So *stubborn*?

She'd thought of going to New York, finding him, demanding more answers. Yet what answers were there that he hadn't already given? She just didn't like them.

She hated them.

Zoe closed her eyes. It wasn't pride that kept her from returning to New York; she had none left. It wasn't even fear, because the worst had already happened.

It was despair.

Funny, how she could think she was doing fine, that she was happy, only to be utterly swamped by despair.

Zoe opened her eyes. And blinked. Then she blinked again. There was a figure standing at the end of the drive.

Even as her heart lurched in wild hope, she told herself that it was improbable. Impossible. Max Monroe had not—could not, would not—travel to England to find her. And even if he did, he wouldn't walk up her driveway like some returning soldier of war.

He'd drive up in his damned limo.

Yet who was it? Who could it be? Zoe struggled to her feet, her heart starting to beat with steady, heavy thuds. The figure was drawing closer, and there was something terribly wonderful about the slow, deliberate strides he was making. Zoe took a few faltering steps down the drive, one hand stretched out of its own accord, in supplication…and then she stopped.

She could see now it was Max, and she knew instinctively this was one journey he needed to make all on his own.

Yet it seemed to take an age for him to walk the drive; Zoe knew it was a quarter of a mile, yet it felt as if he were crossing the Sahara. She thought of how unfamiliar everything must be to him, how strange and perhaps scary, so many uncertain bumps and turns, and yet still he walked. When he was close enough so she could see his face, she saw he was smiling and she let out a little cry of joy.

Max came to a halt a few feet away from her. 'I smell roses,' he said.

'They're in bloom, everywhere—'

'No, it's more like rose water. It's you.'

'It's my shampoo actually.'

Max smiled. 'I thought that's what it was.'

They remained silent, standing, and Zoe felt the words bloom inside her, ready to burst right out of her. *You came. You found me. I love you.* Yet somehow she kept them back and waited for Max to speak.

'I'm sorry,' Max said finally, 'for putting you through so much hell.'

A little bubble of laughter escaped her. Forgiveness was easy. 'Apology accepted.'

'It shouldn't be that easy.'

'I told you before—it doesn't have to be hard.'

Max was silent for a long moment; the sun beat down on both of their heads. 'I suppose that's what I'm afraid of,' he said quietly. 'That it's going to be too hard...for me.'

'I'll be with you.'

'I don't want to fail. I don't want to fail you.'

Zoe blinked hard. 'You won't, Max, because you love me. We can be strong together.'

Max was silent again. 'I thought I sent you away because I was protecting you. Doing the honourable thing. But you were right, Zoe. It was fear. I was afraid. I still am.'

'So am I,' she whispered. 'It's OK.'

'It was hell getting here,' Max said. A smile flickered around his mouth. 'I did it the hard way, to test myself. The subway, the airport and then a bus to Balfour village. I walked the rest.'

She let out a little disbelieving laugh. 'You really do like to put yourself through the mill. You could have at least taken a taxi to the airport.'

He laughed, and suddenly, wonderfully, he snatched her into his arms, buried his face in her hair. Zoe's arms came around him, revelling in his familiar strength. 'I'm so sorry,' he whispered against her hair, his lips pressed to her brow. 'I'm so sorry.'

And Zoe knew he was… Sorry for everything, from the moment on the beach when he'd sent her away, her hopes and heart in ashes, to the afternoon in his office when he'd told her he couldn't be involved in their baby's life, to the morning after they made love. Even before that, she suspected, to the mistakes he felt he'd made nineteen years ago, the mistakes whose repercussions could be felt even now.

'I forgive you, Max,' she whispered. 'I forgive you and I love you.' She drew back then, her hands cupping his face, staring deep into those dark grey eyes. He looked back, and Zoe knew he could see her. Perhaps not with his eyes, but with his heart. She kissed him then, sweetly, deeply, conveying all the hope and love and happiness she felt deep inside, wanting him to feel it too. And when he kissed her back, she knew he did—and more.

Finally they broke apart and, smiling, Zoe reached for Max's hand. 'Come inside,' she said, 'and meet my father.'

When sensible Annie Balfour attends an exclusive
business conference in Italy, her heart skips a beat.
Her mysterious business partner is none other than
Luca de Salvatore—the one man she never expected to see
again and the father of her secret child!

Powerful billionaire Luca *always* gets what he wants. And
he'll make no exception when it comes to
claiming his heir and taking Annie as his wife!

Turn the page for a sneak peek at

Annie's Secret

by

Carole Mortimer

Available January 2012
in WHSmith

ANNIE'S SECRET

"Have your friends all deserted you…?"

Annie, having been gazing apprehensively down the Italian mountain slope, trying to decide whether she felt up to the risk of skiing down her first black run, now felt a quiver down her spine that owed nothing to the danger of the slope or the chill in the air and everything to the sound of that huskily accented voice that spoke so teasingly behind her.

That quiver turned to a delicious shiver as she turned and took her first look at the man who had spoken. Very tall, and dressed all in black, with wide shoulders and narrow waist and hips, he looked like one of those male models her older sister Bella so often worked with. Except there was nothing in the least false or affected about this man's raw sexuality.

Black reflective sunglasses prevented Annie from seeing what colour his eyes were, but the rest of him certainly took her breath away. Shoulder-length dark hair showed beneath his woollen ski-hat, the face behind the sunglasses was tanned, with high cheekbones and a long aristocratic nose above a sensually chiselled mouth, and his square jaw was strong and determined.

He gave her a devilish grin, his teeth very white and even against the dark swarthiness of his skin. "Or perhaps you simply changed your mind about attempting this particular run?" he taunted.

That was exactly what Annie *had* done!

She hadn't been too sure if she wanted to come on this holiday when a dozen or so of her university friends had suggested they all go on a post-Christmas skiing trip to Italy before they settled down to studying for their final exams in the summer, but surprisingly the last week had been a lot of fun. The weather had been perfect. The skiing fantastic. And there had been a noisy party in their chalet every night, usually with lots of other guests staying at the resort invited to join them.

After years of suffering the fierce competitiveness of her sisters when they went on their annual winter holiday to Klosters, Annie had found herself blossoming in the more relaxed company of her friends. So much so, that today, with only three days of her holiday left to go, she had decided to attempt a black run. Unfortunately she had chickened out after the last of her friends had already set off to join the others for hot chocolate in the cafeteria at the bottom of the mountain.

Only to now find herself being challenged by this gorgeous Italian...

"I was just taking a breather," she excused, not quite truthfully.

He flashed her a hard, knowing smile. "Then perhaps you would care to join me in a race to the bottom?"

And perhaps she wouldn't! It would be foolish, totally reckless, to accept this gorgeous man's challenge.

Wouldn't it...?

Foolish *and* reckless, Annie acknowledged. But, after being practical and sensible all her life, wasn't it time she did something foolish and reckless – like following this sexily attractive man down a mountain? Of course it was!

Annie straightened determinedly. "That's fine with me!" She dug her poles into the soft snow to push herself forward onto the run.

An experienced if only competent skier, Annie was no match for the skill of the man who overtook her within seconds of them setting off, his style much more daring than her own as he 'hot-dogged' down the mountain ahead of her.

Needing all her concentration just to remain upright, Annie nevertheless found herself watching the sheer elegance of the man's style. He moved so smoothly, so capably, that just looking at him was exhilarating and, by the time she skied to a halt beside him at the bottom of the mountain, her cheeks were flushed and her eyes a bright periwinkle blue.

"That was fun!" She laughed up at him breathlessly.

"Yes, it was." He gave her another of those devil-may-care smiles as he removed his sunglasses to reveal the deepest, darkest brown eyes Annie had ever looked into.

"Want to try it again?" she suggested enthusiastically, reluctant for this time with him to end. With three beautiful sisters older than her, Annie rarely found herself the object of any man's interest, let alone one as gorgeous as this one.

The man grinned down at her. "I have finished skiing for today and now it is my intention to return to my chalet and drink schnapps."

The light went out of the young woman's deep

blue eyes, her smile becoming noticeably disappointed. "Oh."

He looked down at her speculatively. "Perhaps you would care to join me?" he asked.

"I would?" She blinked up at him owlishly. "I mean —Yes, I would." She gave a firm nod.

"Luc." He removed his ski glove before proffering his hand.

She returned the gesture, her hand small and warm in his much larger one. "Annie."

Special thanks and acknowledgement are given to Carole Mortimer for her contribution to The Balfour Legacy series

A sneaky peek at next month...

MODERN™

INTERNATIONAL AFFAIRS, SEDUCTION & PASSION GUARANTEED

My wish list for next month's titles...

In stores from 16th December 2011:

❑ The Man Who Risked It All – Michelle Reid

❑ The End of her Innocence – Sara Craven

❑ Secrets of Castillo del Arco – Trish Morey

❑ Untouched by His Diamonds – Lucy Ellis

In stores from 6th January 2012:

❑ The Sheikh's Undoing – Sharon Kendrick

❑ The Talk of Hollywood – Carole Mortimer

❑ Hajar's Hidden Legacy – Maisey Yates

❑ The Secret Sinclair – Cathy Williams

❑ Say It with Diamonds – Lucy King

Available at WHSmith, Tesco, Asda, Eason, Amazon and Apple

Visit us Online

You can buy our books online a month before they hit the shops! **www.millsandboon.co.uk**

1211/01